11/13

Spaghetti Rain

Joan Trotter Srager

iUniverse LLC
Bloomington

Spaghetti Rain

iUniverse books may be ordered through booksellers or by contacting:

*iUniverse
1663 Liberty Drive
Bloomington, IN 47403
www.iuniverse.com
1-800-Authors (1-800-288-4677)*

*ISBN: 978-1-4917-0515-5 (sc)
ISBN: 978-1-4917-0514-8 (hc)
ISBN: 978-1-4917-0513-1 (e)*

Library of Congress Control Number: 2013915171

Printed in the United States of America.

iUniverse rev. date: 9/30/2013

Table of Contents

Dedication

For my daughters, Pamela Simon and Elisa Kilgren; my grandchildren, Jessica, Stephanie, Jordan, and Alexis; and my husband, Leslie, without whose help and encouragement this novel would have remained locked within me. To Grandmother Rachael, whose spirit has guided me in writing this book.

Chapter 1

My Best Friend

September 7, 1949

Dear RR:

I will be entering high school at age thirteen, five months, instead of fourteen, so I need to grow up fast. I was pushed ahead in the sixth grade because I did so well on the IQ test. If I'd known that would happen, I'd have tried to catch some disease like leprosy. The truth is, RR, I'm not ready to leave a school I've known from kindergarten through eighth grade. I'm not ready to attend a large high school, where I've been told there are tough girls who hang out in the bathrooms, and I use the bathroom a lot. Also, my body is not ready. Where are the breasts my friends are starting to sprout? Where is the "curse"? It hasn't visited me yet.

And I'm a tomboy. Boys only like the pretty girls with pointed bras and swishy skirts. They get the stares when they walk down the street. Do I stay a tomboy because I don't feel pretty, especially with a metal cap on my front tooth? But it's fun being a tomboy, and part of me likes being different than the popular girls. What should I do?

This is my first entry, RR, and the first day of the last year at my school. Your initials stand for Ruthie's Reflections. I've decided to write only about the year 1949-50,

1

the beginning of my teen years. I'm going to reflect on a day or days each month that make me feel I'm becoming more grown-up-ready to face George Washington High School. Let's face it, RR, I have no other place to go. My parents can't afford a private school.

So here I am, a skinny, flat-chested twelve-year-old tomboy with a metal front tooth, starting my last year at a school I love and afraid of the new school I'll have to attend next fall. You'll be my best friend, RR–the friend I can really talk to. I'll hide you on the top shelf of my closet. Someday I'll show you to my children and grandchildren. I want them to know what I thought and felt when I was just beginning my grown-up years. I believe, RR, you're going to be an important part of my life.

September 23, 1949–our apartment
Dear RR:
I looked up teenager in the dictionary. A teenager is an adolescent, a high school student, a young man or young woman. It's the last definition that interests me. A young woman! I pledge to you, RR, I'll try to be more of a young woman before I start high school, but I bet it won't be as much fun as being a tomboy–unless I meet a cute boy. That could change things.

Right now I'm really in trouble. I did a childish thing this afternoon. My father, "the Volcano," a word that describes his temper, is going to erupt when he hears about the stupid thing I did at lunch. I wish I could talk to my father and tell him I'm sorry, but he's always too busy shouting to listen to me. Will he ever let me grow up? Do I want to grow up? Maybe I'm not cut out to be a "young woman."

Chapter 2

Today It Rained Spaghetti with Red Sauce

My aunts on my mother's side call my father "Joe the Volcano." They say he's a force of nature, and you never know when he's going to erupt. Maybe that's because he was born in 1906, the year of the San Francisco earthquake. He'll erupt tonight when he finds out what I did at lunch. Even my mother can't do anything with him when he blows up. Still, I wish Mother would come home from her job as a saleswoman at Gimbels department store on Thirty-Fourth Street. My father sells shoes at Footrest, a woman's shoe store on the same street. The subway, which my father takes to and from work, will be steamy. He's crankier when he's hot and tired. Too bad today is not Thursday, when my father works until 9:00 p.m. It's Friday, though. He'll be home by six—too soon for me. I wish I didn't have to go home.

The pavement burns my feet through the soles of my sandals as I walk the two long blocks home from school. I race past Mrs. Hamft, leaning on a pillow on her first-floor window ledge.

"Hello, Ruthie," she yells out at me, "give your *mother* my love!" I hear her bellow as I hurry to our building. "How she puts up with your father, I'll ..." Her words trail off as I near the entrance.

When I step into the dimly lit lobby, I spot our upstairs neighbor, Mrs. Green, waiting for the elevator. Just seeing Mrs. Green *piques* me. (Piqued is my new vocabulary word this week.) She never says a nice thing about anyone, and she smells like chopped liver. It's hard not to stare at Mrs. Green. One upright black hair protrudes from a large, black mole above her lip. The mole with its upright hair moves like an antenna caught in the wind whenever Mrs. Green speaks.

My friend Karen once described our lobby décor as "neogrotesque." An enormous gilded mirror hangs in a wall recess. Our Gothic lobby makes a perfect backdrop for a Frankenstein horror movie. I picture the monster creeping up behind Mrs. Green. Seeing him makes the hair in her mole quiver.

She lives in the apartment directly above ours. Every Friday we hear her chop liver through our kitchen ceiling for their Sabbath dinner. I'm Jewish on my mother's side, but we never celebrate the Sabbath. Mrs. Green and I step into the elevator. "I'm going to the basement to get my wash," she says and presses "B," adding, "Give my love to your mother!"

I'm glad to have the elevator to myself so I can turn over on the bars. I hold onto them where they meet at right angles, walk my feet up the wall, and flip. My skirt covers my head, exposing my underpants. It's lucky that no one else rings for the elevator. I know I'm too old to flip, but it's so much fun. If someone saw me I would just die. This has to be my last flip. I'm going to be thirteen this April. That is, if I make it to thirteen after my father finds out what happened.

It began this afternoon when Karen walked home with me for lunch break from school. Mother had left last night's spaghetti in the refrigerator, but Karen and I weren't in the mood for spaghetti. "If we hurry we can grab some hot dogs and pickles from Lennie's deli and get back to school before lunch break ends," I said.

"Let's chuck it out the kitchen window. The alley cats will eat the spaghetti, so it won't be wasted," Karen suggested. It seemed like a good idea at the time.

I opened the window as wide as too many paint jobs would allow and tossed out the spaghetti reddened with tomato sauce. How was I to know that Mrs. O'Brien, who lives in the apartment right below us, would lean out the window to shake her mop at the very moment the spaghetti was falling? Mrs. O'Brien's hair, white blouse, arms, and mop were covered with cold, red spaghetti.

"Glad Mrs. O'Brien is a redhead," Karen whispered to me. We tried not to giggle as we snuck away from the window. We tore down the staircase across the hall from our apartment. All the way to the deli we laughed. I stopped laughing when I pictured Mrs. O'Brien telling the super it was "raining spaghetti" from apartment 4J. My hot dog tasted like cardboard, even with sauerkraut piled on top.

With the vision of Mrs. O'Brien covered with red-sauced spaghetti on my mind, I stumble out of the elevator on the fourth floor.

I sing the words to "Playmates," a song my mother used to sing to me when I was a little girl and something scared me:

> Playmates,
> Come out and play with me,
> And bring your dollies three.
> Climb up my apple tree
> And we shall be friends
> Forever more.

The song usually makes me feel better, but not today. Like flipping over an elevator handrail, I'm getting too old for "Playmates." I look out the hall window to the alley below. I don't see an apple tree. I don't see any spaghetti either. Probably the cats ate it. Maybe my father will believe me if I tell him someone in another J-line apartment made spaghetti rain out the window at the same time I was home for lunch. Maybe my father will have developed a sense of humor overnight and find it funny. Maybe he won't explode. Maybe ...

I turn the key in the lock of our apartment. No one is home—yet!

September 23, 7:00 p.m—our apartment
Dear RR:

I've never seen my father so angry. He scared me tonight. I know he loved me when I was a kid. Does he still now that I'm growing up? I don't know. But I do know this. I hate it when he yells and frightens me. Right now I don't love my father, and that's not a good feeling.

Chapter 3

The Volcano Erupts

My eyes are glued to my parents' bedroom window facing the street. I'm on the lookout for my father. I can't concentrate on Nancy Drew, *The Ghost of Blackwood Hall*. Abandoning the window, I visit Grandma Rachael—her photograph that is. She died years before I was born.

Grandma looks strong. I bet she could calm the Volcano. Aunt Edith, Mother's sister, is the only living person who can cool down my father. He listens to her. But she lives in Florida.

Although Mother usually can't do anything with my father when he explodes, I wish she was home. Looking out the window again, I see my father strutting down the block, a rolled newspaper clutched in his hand for protection (probably from our neighbors). His shirt collar is unbuttoned; his polka dot bow tie is untied. His pinstriped suit jacket hangs over one shoulder. As he closes in on our building, I see that his shirt sticks to his back. "*Where'd you learn how to park a car?*" he barks to a neighbor who is backing unsuccessfully into a tight parking spot.

His footsteps echo as he walks down the hall toward our apartment. His keys clink while he tries to find the apartment key.

"Hi, Dad," I say, when he finally opens the door. He doesn't answer. He marches straight to the bedroom to change his clothes. He bangs the soap against the sink when he washes up in the bathroom. Still without a word, he goes into the kitchen. I turn off the water he's left running in the sink.

Why is he so angry? Because of the spaghetti rain? Did the super speak to him about it? Or did Mrs. O'Brien? Maybe Mrs. O'Brien cut off some of her hair with spaghetti sticking to it and carried her stained shirt as evidence. Maybe he's only had a bad day at work. I picture him surrounded by stacks of shoes he's dragged up the stairs from the basement. I picture ladies trying on shoes but not buying a pair. That may be it. I try to calm myself.

My father scrapes a carrot in the kitchen. He fills a glass with a shot of scotch, adds ice and club soda, and plunks down the carrot and the drink on a snack table next to his chair in the living room. Every evening before dinner he has one scotch and soda. His evening ritual!

From his chair, my father surveys his empire. A red sofa bed, where I sleep, stands across from a mahogany breakfront flanked by Mother's chair. An alcove outside of the living area carves out room for a black leather table and four black chairs with gray leather seats. The set, framed by long mirrors attached to the wall, belonged to Aunt Mary, Mother's sister. I wait for him to set up the checkers we often play before dinner, but he doesn't.

I go into the kitchen and set the table for dinner. Then I hear the hall door open. "Hi, honey," says Mother, giving me a hug. "Can't wait to get out of my girdle." Then she whispers, "Is your father grumpy?" I shake my head yes.

"Maybe a good dinner will put him in a better mood."

"I defrosted the fish he caught last Sunday and cooked beets this morning."

My chair in the kitchen is in front of the window facing the alley, next to the heating pipe. No way out!

"Dad," I blurt, "Karen came over this afternoon to have lunch with me."

"There was enough spaghetti and sauce for the two of you," Mother volunteers.

Dad purses his lips. "Get to the point," he demands. "I'm meeting Sollie at the newsstand," his first words of the evening.

"Well, Karen and I took the spaghetti from the refrigerator. We were dying for hot dogs and pickles from Lennie's, so we threw it out the kitchen window—the spaghetti, that is ..."

"*You did what?*" my father shouts.

"We figured it would land at the bottom of the alley, and the cats would eat it. But how were we to know Mrs. O'Brien would be shaking out her dust mop at just the wrong time. Mom's spaghetti and tomato sauce landed on her blouse, arms, and mop. Some got on her hair, too."

A giggle percolates. I pray to the giggle god to choose someone else tonight.

"Daddy, I wanted to tell you before the super does." I never call him Daddy anymore, but I thought it wouldn't hurt to remind him I'm only twelve years old.

"*Before the super tells me,*" he yells at me, turning beet-red.

I feel my father's anger across the table. I stare at my plate. "Mrs. O'Brien figured out the spaghetti dropped from 4J since it came from directly above her. She probably told the super," I murmur, fingering my napkin.

He sputters, "*Mrs. O'Brien is still angry because I hit her on the arm with a stray pea from my peashooter. I was shooing away the pigeons. I told her I'd make her a peashooter, but she slammed down her window and hasn't spoken to me since.*"

I mumble under my breath, "Hardly anyone in the building speaks to you."

Weapons of my father's war against the pigeons wait on the counter next to the meat grinder. I eye the wooden slingshot my father carved with his three-blade knife, and the container of dried peas he uses with the slingshot to shoot at the pigeons that gossip on our kitchen window sill or in the alley. I bite my tongue trying not to giggle at the thought of that pea smacking against Mrs. O'Brien's arm.

"She sure gets a lot of food from this apartment," I whisper.

My father roars, *"Don't get fresh with me, whatever you're saying, Ruth. How could you do such a thing? Throwing food out the window? Didn't you see her leaning out? I bet she told all the neighbors."*

My father bangs his glass of water on the table. It spills over the plastic tablecloth. He grabs the bowl of beets and flings it across the room. He's never thrown anything before. The bowl crashes against the white-tiled wall and shatters into pieces. Beet juice bleeds down the tile onto the black-and-white linoleum floor.

He glares at me. My father has never hit me, but tonight he raises his hand, and I flinch. Mother jumps in front of me. I feel her body trembling like mine. He slams out of the apartment, banging the door shut. Flakes of ceiling paint land on the hall rug.

Silence fills the kitchen. Mother puts her arms around me and cradles me. "I hate him! I hate him!" I wail. Then my mother and I begin to clean up the mess.

I don't see my father until breakfast. He is dressed for work and smells of Old Spice aftershave. No one says a word for what seems forever.

"I don't want Mrs. O'Brien and the neighbors in the building thinking Joe Treglia is raising a brat. You go and apologize after breakfast. Oh, and tell her I'll fillet some fish for her on Sunday after I go fishing."

"Okay, Dad," I say as he leaves the apartment. He doesn't look back at me. Mother and I clear off the breakfast dishes. "How can you stay married to him?" I ask her.

She throws her arms around me. "That's just his way, Ruthie," she replies in her soft voice. "He's Italian—quick-tempered. It blows over as quickly as it blows up. You know he loves you," Mother says, holding me so tightly I can hear her heart beating.

"He has some way of showing it," I say, pulling away. "Why can't he just scold me? Maybe then I could tell him I know I was wrong and that I'll try not to be so stupid."

"He doesn't know how to do that, but he was calm this morning and worked out what should be done."

"Does it always have to be his way? If he had given me a chance I'd have told him I'd apologize to Mrs. O'Brien and help her carry her groceries or something. How does he expect me to grow up if he doesn't let me think for myself?"

"Maybe he's afraid to let you grow up." I look at my mother. Is she right? Is my father afraid for me to grow up and have opinions of my own?

Later my father comes home with a window fan in a carton. On Sunday afternoon, he installs it in the bottom of the kitchen window. The slingshot and the container of peas have vanished from their home next to the meat grinder. I think my father and I will miss them and that open window.

October 11, 1949—the woods
Dear RR:

 The days are getting shorter, and I want to remember this afternoon with my friend Karen in our hideout in the woods near her apartment. Soon we'll be off to different schools and different friends. Hanging out together is coming to a close. So, maybe, is being a tomboy.

Chapter 4

The Days Are Getting Shorter

Karen is my tomboy friend. Her parents are divorced. Sometimes I wish my parents were, especially when they argue. I haven't forgotten last month when my father smashed a bowl of beets against the wall. It'd be much calmer living only with Mother, although I don't imagine living with Karen's mother would be calm. She's strict about everything. Mrs. Klein, Karen's mother, is a substitute teacher in our school. We don't fool around when she subs. She handles the classroom as if it's a Communist labor camp.

"There is *no* talking in my classroom!"

"If you haven't done your homework—*no* recess!"

"If you do not finish *all* your morning work—*no* recess!"

Karen called Mrs. Klein "Mother" once in class by mistake. She tore up Karen's paper right in front of everybody.

It smells like fall this afternoon. There's a chill in the air. During recess, kids and teachers listen to the World Series on portable radios.

We only have a few hours of light after school until our parents want us home. I rub my hands over my dark-brown suede jacket bibbed with fringes. Karen owns the same jacket, except in red. No one in our grade has jackets like ours. We like to be different. In class we wink at each other knowing what we plan to do after school. This morning I hid my tomboy clothes under the stairwell off the lobby in our building. I hope no one took them.

Karen and I are *part-time* tomboys because we have to wear skirts or dresses to school and when we're out with our parents. Once we put on our dungarees and tuck our hair under our caps, we *transform* into tomboys, sort of like Superman, who is boring Clark Kent most of the time except when he has to save Lois Lane. We stuff our hands into our pockets. We take longer strides when we walk down the sidewalks.

Today, after school, as we head across the street to Karen's building, she announces, "I'm never going to wear makeup, not even lipstick. When I grow up, I want to be an airplane pilot."

I want to be a writer or a ballet dancer, but I keep the ballet part to myself. Karen thinks ballet lessons are for sissies. Can a tomboy be a ballet dancer? Karen would laugh at me. "I'll never get my hair colored or wear a bra. Not that that matters. I'll *never* have breasts," I tell Karen as I get into tomboy mood.

"First you have to get your period, stupid. Gosh, don't you know anything?" Karen teases me just before we enter the lobby of her modern building. Inside her apartment, Karen promises to steal her maid Virgie's sexy cartoon strips to teach me the facts of life. I stare at the floor. Mother doesn't tell me anything about becoming a woman.

"What's sexy about a cartoon strip anyway?" I ask. "What's sexy about Prince Valiant or Archie and Veronica?"

"*These* cartoons are dirty," Karen informs me. "There's a doctor who makes a house call. He does *it* with his pretty patient who's in bed wearing a see-through negligee. The doctor carries a black bag. He takes a stethoscope from it and places it on her breast."

I'm never going to look at a doctor's bag in the same way.

"Dr. Belsky never seemed dirty to me when he used a stethoscope," I comment.

"That's because you're not sexy," Karen says, laughing as we head to the bedroom she shares with her sister. How great it must be to have a room separate from your parents, a room to share with a sister—to have a sister! Their bathroom is in the hall. Mrs. Klein has a full bath in her bedroom. Two bedrooms and two bathrooms!

Karen sheds her skirt for a pair of dungarees. Her black, curly hair disappears under a boy's cap with earflaps. Leaving her building, we gallivant down the two blocks to my building. Under the stairwell, I reach for the bag I've hidden. Karen is my lookout. I shimmy into the dungarees, shove my skirt into my schoolbag, and cover my light-brown, wavy hair with a wool cap. The bag with my school clothes is stowed back under the stairs. Mother's visiting Aunt Mary today. I have to change back into my school clothes before my parents get home.

"Boys are so lucky. They get to dress like this all the time. They can climb, fight, and get dirty, and no one cares," Karen complains.

Across the street I see two of the popular girls. Their pointy bras push against their angora sweaters like medieval weapons. They wear skirts, barrettes in their pageboys, and bright-red lipstick. They flirt with two boys, one being Harold Meister. Every girl has a crush on Harold—even we do. "Who cares?" Karen answers in a voice loud enough to hear across the street. "So the boys like how they look. Big deal! They don't have any fun." But I care that they laugh at us. I feel ashamed of how I look right now, but I keep those thoughts to myself.

We take long strides to Lennie's. We saunter up the block on our way to the woods, scarfing down our hot dogs with sauerkraut and crunching on sour pickles.

"We'd better hurry up if we want to have time in the woods before it gets dark," I warn.

"I'll race you," Karen shouts back at me, already ahead and dodging people on the block. We could take a path off Fort Tryon Park to get into the woods, but what fun would that be? I catch up with her by the time we get to the *fire hatch,* our nickname for a narrow tree with brown bark that we slide down to enter the woods below street level. To grab onto the hatch we must climb on a stone wall and jump about one foot to reach the tree. It's a three-foot fall to the bottom of the woods if we miss the tree.

We run, tripping over brambles, until we come to the hideout, a clearing we've been transforming into ours. We've hidden our stuff in the hollow of a tree: two pocket knives, marshmallows, flashlights, and safety matches wrapped in a plastic bag to keep them dry. Two fallen trees are the right height for benches. This is also a great place to practice our climbing. We scramble up a nearby tree and hang out in the lower branches. From there we can see the West Side Highway and the Hudson River across to New Jersey.

"Hey, we could start a small club and have some kind of initiation rites here," I suggest. It's fun making plans with Karen. She's up for anything. But we'll be graduating this year. We won't be starting anything. I'll be walking over a mile to George Washington High School, and Karen will take the subway to Calhoun, a private high school downtown. We're going to meet different kids, and I've a feeling we're not going to be best friends anymore. "Karen, this may be the last year you and I will be fooling around in the woods."

"Yeah, I know," Karen says, taking some stones and pitching them toward the river. "The hideout will seem silly when we're in high school."

We make a small fire in a pit with dry twigs. We toast some of the marshmallows with two long sticks. Charred bits of marshmallow cling to our mouths. We try to wipe the marshmallow off with our dirty hands, but mud from the woods paints our faces like makeup.

"Let's practice 'Territory,'" Karen suggests, a game we play with boys in our class in the empty lot near school. We carve a circle in the dirt with our pocket knives and divide the pie into two pieces, taking turns carving up the pie. Whoever ends up with the whole pie wins the game.

"It's more fun when we're playing with boys," Karen says with a yawn.

"How about going over to where they're putting up the new building?" I propose. We throw dirt on the fire to smother it. It's harder to climb up the fire hatch than slide down. We have to wrap our legs around the tree and inch our way up, the way we do when we climb the ropes in gym. We're even more of a mess by the time we scramble back onto Cabrini Boulevard. The scratches on our faces and hands are crisscrossed with dirt.

We dash down to the new building two blocks away. A bunch of boys are climbing up the scaffolding and jumping off the unfinished second floor.

"Look at the dirty tomboys," the boys tease. "Bet you're chicken to jump off the second floor!"

Karen and I raise our eyebrows. A dare is a dare! We climb up the scaffolding, walk to the edge, and let out a whoop. We jump together. Luckily, the mud and branches soften our fall, but we're more scratched up and dirty than when we left the woods. We turn to the boys and flap our wings like chickens, brush ourselves off, and race up the block. "I'll smuggle Virgie's cartoons out of the house, and we can look at them after school," Karen shouts, smiling and waving good-bye.

Today my father will be home at six; I have to beat him and change my clothes. He's still angry with me. Mrs. O'Brien doesn't talk to him. I run pretty fast without a skirt holding me back. I wonder if even Karen had as much fun in our hideout as we used to. Something was different. Something felt off.

I loved jumping off the second floor like the boys. I'll always want to try things that scare me. I want to keep that tomboy part of me. Why can't a grown-up have fun too—just in a different way? But I'm still scared of high school. Jumping off the second story of a building isn't going to help me there. I brush away some dead leaves caught in the fringes of my jacket.

October 19, 1949–Nicole's apartment
Dear RR:

I want a different type of marriage than my parents if I get married at all. Movies usually end when the two stars have fallen in love, have overcome setbacks, and have finally come together. What happens afterward—when they've been married for a while? That's what interests me.

Chapter 5

An Arranged Marriage
and an Affair

On Wednesday afternoons, my friends, Anna, Gaby and I spend the afternoon at Nicole's apartment because that's when her mother, Mrs. Girard, meets a friend. A red leather belt cinches a print dress around Mrs. Girard's narrow waist. "Take off your shoes, girls," she instructs us, as she bundles herself in a black Persian lamb coat, a sprig of red cherries pinned to the collar. "I'll be home late, but dinner is in the refrigerator. Don't wait for me. I'm not sure when I'll be back," she says, her French accent making her sound exotic. Mrs. Girard smiles good-bye and leaves us with the scent of Chanel perfume.

"How *sumptuous* your mother looks," I say to Nicole. "You have your mother's beautiful skin and high cheekbones."

Anna looks at Nicole and raises one eyebrow. They're sharing some secret about Mrs. Girard, but as usual I'm clueless as to what's going on. I ask Anna why she looked at Nicole that way. Anna shrugs her shoulders and says, "What way?"

Mrs. Girard has an arranged marriage. Her parents arranged the marriage because it was the custom for her family to select a suitable husband for their daughter. She is twenty years younger than her husband. Grandmother

Rachael used to arrange marriages for relatives and friends from the "old country," Mother informed me when I questioned Mrs. Girard's marriage.

Mr. Girard was in the diamond business in France and was considered a *good catch*. I hate that expression. As if you can reel in a husband the way my father reels in a fish. Marry someone you hardly know—maybe will never love? No one is going to catch a husband for me or arrange a marriage. I want to be in love like Jeanne Crain was with her husband, William Holden, in the movie *Apartment for Peggy*, in which she helped him through college on his small GI Bill checks.

Stepping on the thick plastic that covers the foyer rug, we crunch by the *drop* living room, a few feet lower than the foyer. Through the double-paned window in the back of the living room I see the woods where Karen and I have our hideout, and beyond that the Hudson River. I linger behind to admire the Girard's sumptuous Limoges candlesticks, hand-painted with tiny rose flowers, posing on top of a table in the center of the living room.

"Ruthie, what's taking you so long?" Nicole calls to me.

"I'm just ogling those *sumptuous* candlesticks," I reply as I swoosh along the foyer.

"Stop using that word," my friends scream. "Can't you speak like everyone else?"

"Harold's the type to have an affair when he's older," Anna and Nicole remark at the same time. Anna sneaks a glance at Nicole, who blushes. That's the second time I notice something going on between Nicole and Anna. I wish I knew what.

"An affair! What's an affair?"

"Really, Ruthie!" Anna, Nicole, and Gaby shout in unison. All of them speaking like one is beginning to annoy me.

"You're such a baby," Anna says, staring at my flat chest. "I have to teach you everything."

"An affair is when you go out with someone who is not your husband or wife," Nicole informs me.

"You mean like going to the movies together?"

"It means doing *it* together," Anna answers in her grown-up voice. She seems so much older than me even though she's only thirteen. That's probably because she has a sister who's sixteen and explains things to her.

Gaby begs, "Nicole, you told me your parents have a sex manual for married couples. Please, please look for it."

"I'll get into trouble."

"C'mon, Nicole," Anna says. "Ruthie has to know about *it*. You're doing this for Ruthie. It's our duty as her friends."

Arm in arm we walk into her parents' bedroom, singing, "Friends, friends, we will always be." Anna volunteers to be the lookout in case Nicole's sister returns home. We search for the *good* illustrations in the book. I look for a black leather bag. Karen showed me Virgie's book of sexy cartoons. Ever since, I am wary of men toting black bags that look like doctor's bags. I'm embarrassed to ask my friends about the black bag thing. But I haven't seen the good stuff in the sex manual yet, and maybe that will clear it up.

We hear a sound coming from Nicole's bedroom windows. We run over to the window. It's Karen, back from visiting her father. She's standing in the woods outside Nicole's bedroom window throwing stones. That's just like her. Why ring a doorbell when you can throw stones at a window? I press the book cover against the pane, but Nicole grabs it. She's afraid her sister will come home and tell her mother what we've been doing.

"Wait for me! I'll be right up. I don't want to miss this," Karen shouts as she scrambles up the hill toward the building. As we wait for her, I wonder what a good marriage is. Nicole's mother married a much older man in an arranged marriage. Karen's parents are divorced and hate each other. My father yells at my mother. And I'd never marry someone as conceited as Harold. Besides he might have an affair, and I know now what that is. If I marry, I want it to be to someone who is gentle and adores only me and who thinks about important stuff.

I don't think I'm going to find out everything I want to know about marriage in Nicole's parents' sex manual, and certainly not in Virgie's cartoons. But I do know that I want my marriage to be *sumptuous!* I keep my thoughts to myself. I need to figure out that stuff on my own.

November 9, 1949–Gaby's apartment
Dear RR:

I now know my friends left more than their homes when they had to get out of Europe. I can't imagine armed soldiers marching down Fort Washington Avenue. I can't imagine my family packing and taking the train to a boat to … to where? What would we pack? What would we leave behind? I can't understand why no one talks about what happened except in school and newsreels. What I do understand is that I'm a silly girl who complains about silly boys and silly things. I understand why my friends are more mature than I am, and it has nothing to do with growing breasts.

Chapter 6

My Friends Escape
from the Nazis

It's Gaby's turn to have us over after school. I talk to her on the phone every night. I tell her everything. She seems more like my sister than my other friends, maybe because we're both only children. We take turns wearing a pair of small, black enamel earrings we bought at the five-and ten-cent store.

Still dressed in our Assembly Day clothing—orange-popsicle-color ties, white, long-sleeved blouses, and navy-blue pleated skirts—we lounge in Gaby's bedroom. Our loafers with pennies nestled in the smile of the shoe have been tossed on the floor, nearly hitting Gaby's stretching cat.

Right now, we're angry with Harold because he sent the same Valentine's Day card to all the girls in our class.

"You'd think he'd have bought a box of assorted Valentine cards," Gaby complains.

"What do you think of today's assembly?" I ask, anxious to end this depressing discussion about Harold. The principal told us the eighth grade will be studying World War II, and a concentration camp survivor from the neighborhood will speak at next week's assembly about her experiences in Europe. "Did you catch no one was paying attention, and the boys in the back were throwing paper airplanes at each other?" I ask.

Gaby, Nicole, and Anna become very quiet and stare at each other. They're never quiet, especially Anna. They ignore my question.

I'm about to ask them what's wrong when I spot in Gaby's bookcase a book we had read when we were in the first grade.

"Remember this reader, *Fun with Dick and Jane*?" I open the book and pick out a page in which the mother sits on a green club chair, wearing a dress and a pair of white, high-heeled pumps. She cradles her smiling daughter Jane on her lap, a blue ribbon adorning her blonde hair. Jane's brother Dick leans over the chair. The mother is reading the story "Look Up." I read the first three lines in a singsong voice:

> Dick said,
> Look, look.
> Look up.
> Look up, up, up.

"What a dumb book," says Anna. "Who speaks like that?"

"This is an *addlebrained* book," I say. "The whole family is *addlebrained*."

"Didn't they have a dog named Spot and a cat named Puff?" Nicole chimes in. I nod as I flip through the pages. I think of the plastic Mrs. Girard puts over the rug in the foyer and the furniture in the living room. I can't imagine a cat or dog in Nicole's apartment, although I noticed Nicole stroked Gaby's cat.

We stream out of her bedroom and plop on the large, overstuffed couches in the living room. All the furniture in this room is oversized. The dark wood bookcases bulge with books, many written in German. A long oak writing table sandwiched between the two windows, which face front, is piled high with papers and more books. Gaby's name is Gabriela, but she changed it to Gaby because she thinks it sounds more American.

I know some things about Gaby because her mother and my father were wardens during the war. She was born in Germany. Her father owned a factory in Veil, a town named after their family. Now Mr. Veil works in a factory. My father told me they left their home after *Kristallnacht*, the night of broken glass we read about in school last week. Storefront windows of Jewish-owned businesses across Germany were smashed. My father cautioned me not to speak to Gaby about this—that it's best to forget such terrible things. I was shocked my father confided in me. It made me feel proud.

I've overheard my parents whisper in the kitchen a bit about Anna and Nicole. They also escaped *in time*. "In time" means my friends and their families escaped from Europe before they were killed or thrown into camps by the Nazis.

Anna's family fled from Austria to the Philippines, lived through the Japanese invasion of the Philippines, and escaped from there to America.

Nicole's family left France before the Germans invaded in 1940. Last summer her family traveled back to France for the first time since the war. We saw her off on the luxury liner the *Isle de France*.

None of my friends talk about Europe. My parents have never discussed the war with me, except when my father told me about the Veils. In school, we learned that more than six million Jews were killed during World War II, and so were six million other civilians. Such numbers are impossible to imagine.

Even before both world wars, Grandmother Rachael and her family were forced to leave Romania. It seems it has always been hard to be a Jew in Europe. Why are Jews so hated? I'm half-Jewish—would I have been half-hated? Could that happen here? America is where everyone flees to, not from ... right?

I thumb my nose at the foolish "Dick and Jane" book in my hand and declare, "Let's make up our own Dick and Jane stories."

"Great idea, Ruthie," says Anna. Gaby hands out sheets of paper and pens. We sit cross-legged on the floor around the coffee table, munching on pretzels, and drinking Cokes. Since it was my idea, I go first.

I jump on the couch, reciting:

> Dick, quick!
> Sick.
> Sick.
> Sick.

I pretend I'm vomiting and make gagging sounds. Everybody laughs at my sound effects.

Next, Anna stands on the sofa and blasts out:

> Dick touches
> His dick.
> Mom says to Dick,
> No, no, Dick.
> Don't touch dick, Dick.

Anna touches her you-know-what, as she recites her poem. We're laughing so hard tears run down our cheeks. Anna is the one who would say the word "dick." She's been on a date, although her sister and her boyfriend went along.

"Come on, everyone," I say. "Let's write real-life poems." We decide to write about anything we want and to hide our poems from our parents.

26

We sprawl on the carpet, using magazines to support our papers. After about twenty minutes we place the poems on the coffee table. I wonder why my friends are so pale and hushed. I break the silence. "Okay. I'll go first."

> Father
> Yells
> Yells
> Out our window.
> Tells a man
> On the street
> Below, below
> How to park his
> Car, car, car.
> Man says,
> "Look, look, look.
> Up, up, up.
> To the floor on four.
> It's that loud man Joe.
> What a bore."

"Who wants to go next?" I ask, wondering why no one laughed at my poem. After a moment Gaby gets up and stands in front of the window. It gets dark early in February. Behind her the lights glimmer in the apartments across the street. She reads:

> See Dick.
> See Jane.
> See Mom cry.
> See Dad sigh.
> See them run, run, run.
> The Nazis come, come, come.
> See Spot.

"Spot can't come,"
Says Mom.
"Grandma can't run,
But she must come,"
Says Dad, hiding his
Gun, gun, gun.

Nobody says a word. I run to Gaby and squeeze her hand.
"Where did that come from?" Gaby just shakes her head.
Then Nicole stands up in front of the bookcases.

Puff, mon chat,
Au revoir,
Au revoir.
Nicole sails on ship.
Lilot sails on ship.
Mother sails on ship.
Father sails on ship.
Away from war
Away
Away
But *mon chat Puff*
Must stay, stay, stay.

She sinks back onto the couch.
"I've always hated that dumb Dick and Jane family,"
Anna snaps. She jumps up and begins to read, yelling, almost
crying:

The Nazis are dicks.
Tick, tick, tick.
Their bombs are dicks.
This war is sick, sick, sick.
Hitler's the biggest dick of all.

He will fall, fall, fall.
That evil little man
Will never walk
Tall, tall, tall.

"I remember running and hiding in a hole on top of a dead man and being shushed and always feeling hungry," she spits out.

How ignorant I was to make fun of the assembly! How ashamed I feel. I'm about to apologize to my friends when we hear footsteps in the hallway.

"My mom. She's home early!" Gaby cries out. "Hide the poems!"

But we don't have time to hide our poems. They're spread out on the coffee table and the couch as Gaby's mom walks into the living room.

"Hello, girls. What are you up to?" she says, smiling at us. "What are you writing? An English homework assignment?"

Anna says, "We're just writing stuff ... about boys ...." She tries to grab her paper, but it's too late. Mrs. Veil is already reading.

Anna and I shoot looks at each other. I'm sure Anna thinks her "dick" poems are the worst, and I feel the poem about my father is mean, especially since Gaby's mother and my father are still friendly. Mrs. Veil stiffens as she reads Gaby's, Anna's, and Nicole's poems. She brings her hand to her heart. She stares at Gaby. Mrs. Veil seems about to cry, but she collects herself.

"Anna," Mrs. Veil says, "nice girls don't use that word."

Then she turns to me. "I'm going to tear this poem up, Ruthie. I wouldn't want your father to see it." I mutter a quiet thank-you and gather up my books and pea jacket and leave as quickly as I can.

Walking down Fort Tryon Avenue on my way home, I realize I don't know my friends, and I don't know what it means to be Jewish. There are worse things than being embarrassed by my father. And how could I even care about not getting a real Valentine card from Harold Meister!

Back in my apartment, Mother wants to know why I'm so quiet at dinner. I ache to ask her about Grandma Rachael; how she and her family left Romania, but not right now. I'm not sure I can explain the poems written at Gaby's this afternoon, or if I will ever talk about them. Also, I'm angry with my parents. They didn't tell me the truth about my friends.

Before I go to sleep, I take my doll, Tousel, out of her wooden cradle in the back of my closet and bring her to bed with me. I haven't played with her for years. Tousel's glass eyes used to scare me, but they don't anymore. I close my eyes and Dick and Jane, and their mother and father, jump into view. They're goose-stepping, the way the Nazi soldiers did in the newsreels we saw about the war years.

I see the Dick and Jane family tramping behind the soldiers, who are forcing my friends out of their homes to march to the concentration camps. I hear their jeers. I close Tousel's eyes. Then I press her close to me, wetting her face with my tears.

December 25, 1949–Fifth Avenue

Dear RR:

It's Christmas Day. In our apartment we have our own version of Christmas. There's a small fake tree, we open presents by ourselves and eat dinner at a coffee shop near Rockefeller Ice-Skating Rink. We look at the windows decorated for the holidays in the windows of Saks Fifth Avenue. It's as if we rub our fingers over the icing of a cake. We lick a small part of the icing, but never eat the cake. This is the first Christmas I've felt this way. Is it because of what happened at Gaby's when we wrote our poems? I keep hearing boots, but they're not the ones on the feet of the fake Santa Claus ringing a bell on the corner of Fifth Avenue and Fifty-Third Street.

Chapter 7

Giant Red Nutcrackers

The Christmas season starts for me when I send my list to Aunt Edith and Uncle Hy in Miami. Each November my aunt asks me what I want for Christmas, and each year I do the same thing. I ask for everything I want and then add, "Don't buy everything on the list ..." knowing they'll buy everything.

Here's my list:

> a pair of flannel pajamas, a robe and slippers (for sleepovers)
> a nylon blouse, slip, and a taffeta skirt to wear for New Year's Eve (if I'm invited to a party)
> a matching wool hat, scarf, and gloves, preferably in red
> the latest Nancy Drew book, *The Clue of the Leaning Chimney*

Bing Crosby crooning "I'm Dreaming of a White Christmas" and Nat King Cole singing "The Christmas Song" herald the holiday season. A white Christmas is very pretty in the city until the dogs yellow-up the snow banks, and the car exhausts blacken them. I dash downstairs, while the snow is still pure, although Fort Tryon Park stays snow white for a while. "Chestnuts roasting on an open fire ..." is the beginning line of "The Christmas Song." It's hard to imagine chestnuts roasting on an open fire in our apartment. The only fire we had was when Mother burned a hole in her chair. And roasting chestnuts on a radiator isn't the same.

We sing Christmas carols in assembly. My favorite is "Jingle Bells." I try to imagine riding in a one-horse open sleigh. The closest I come is when I ride on my Flexible Flyer sled in Fort Tryon Park.

In assembly, we start to sing, "Hark, the Herald Angels Sing, Glory to our Lord and King," reading the words off a mimeographed song sheet. I'm sitting next to Anna, Nicole, and Gaby. I whisper to them, "How come we never sing any Chanukah songs?" They shrug their shoulders. "Do you know any?" I ask. A teacher tells me to stop talking.

Finally, I'm on Christmas vacation and don't think about Chanukah anymore. My father takes our fake tree from the back corner of the linen closet and places it on the coffee table. We decorate it with tinsel and strung popcorn. A small lopsided rag doll I made years ago straddles the top of the tree. On Christmas Eve, we place presents on the rug under the coffee table. Christmas morning, after opening them, Mother cooks her miniature pancakes and crisp bacon. She whips heavy cream for my parent's coffee and my hot chocolate. I call Aunt Edith and Uncle Hy to thank them for the presents. Of course they bought everything on my list, and all the clothes fit.

After breakfast, my parents and I bundle up, hang our skates with their rubber blade protectors over our jackets, and take the subway to Rockefeller Center. This year's Christmas tree is a Norway spruce, seventy-six feet high, according to the newspaper. That's more than eight times as high as our ceiling! My parents and I go ice-skating at the rink below the tree. We lace up our skates in a small room with a rubber floor off the rink. I'm a pretty good skater, but my parents skate-dance. My father leads, and they glide in step to the

Christmas music; sometimes skating backward, in front of the gilded sculpture of Prometheus, who is supposed to have brought fire to mankind. The onlookers circling the rink from the level above watch them skate. It's a happy time with my father.

A light snow begins to fall, frosting the tree, Prometheus, and the skaters. The tree is dressed with thousands of colored lightbulbs, topped by a white-tipped star reaching for the sky. Christmas music makes me believe that all is at peace with the world. "Good will to all." Isn't that the message of the season, that and buying presents? From Fifth Avenue we can see the Christmas angels blowing their trumpets, heralding the season of joy from their perch on top of Saks Department Store. It's when we walk across the street to look at the windows at Saks—when we pass the giant red nutcrackers in their military uniforms decorating a storefront—that another image bursts into my head.

Storm troopers! I see, I hear, and I feel the Nazi soldiers goose-stepping, dragging terrified men, women, and children to their deaths or off to concentration camps. Off to darkness! The lightness of the day begins to dim. Pieces of my friends' poems come back to me:

Gaby: "See Mom cry, see Dad sigh. See them run, run, run, the Nazis come, come, come ..."

Nicole: Nicole sails on ship ... away from war, away ... but *mon chat Puff* must stay, stay, stay."

Anna: Hitler will fall, fall, fall, that evil little man, will never walk tall, tall, tall."

We're looking through a window at Saks Fifth Avenue. A fairy princess wearing a white-and-silver sparkling dress holds a wand that twinkles. In the background, artificial snowflakes fall behind a revolving Christmas tree. The crowds press against the glass and hold their children up to see the rotating displays. I am spinning too. A hired Santa Claus rings his bell in front of the store. Santa and the window watchers hear me cry out, "*Mother, Dad, why didn't we celebrate Chanukah last week? Why didn't we?*" People turn to stare at us as my parents hurry me away from the store. No one says a word on the way home.

December 26, 1949–our apartment
Dear RR:

I'm ashamed I made a scene in front of the windows at Saks yesterday. I felt rage when I saw the nutcrackers. They're just toy soldiers, one of the many decorations you see at Christmastime. But they made me angry. I hope no one I knew saw me.

Chapter 8

The Wholesale Menorah

The next day, my father returns home from work with a stainless steel, lopsided menorah. "Where'd you get *that* menorah?" I ask.

"Wholesale," he replies, the first word he has said to me since my outburst at the Saks Fifth Avenue windows.

"Where do you get wholesale menorahs?" I ask, picturing stores on the Lower East Side advertising, "Cheapest menorahs in town. Buy here!" This menorah must have fallen out of a thirtieth-floor window. From the look my father gives me I know better than to question him anymore. He also stopped at the Fort Tryon Jewish Center to pick up information sheets about Chanukah. He removes a box of thin colored candles from his coat pocket to use in the menorah.

My father would never say I was right, but I won the Chanukah argument. "I met Mrs. Veil on the subway," my father tells me as he takes off his coat. "She told me about the poems you and your friends wrote the other day." My stomach churns. Did she tell him about all the poems—the one I wrote about him?

"Which poems?" I ask.

"The ones your friends wrote about escaping from Europe." Thank you, Mrs. Veil.

"Chanukah was last week, Dad."

"I know, but we'll celebrate it tomorrow after work."

"We'll exchange a small present each," Mother says, coming into the kitchen, "and I'll make some potato pancakes—latkes—the way Grandma Rachael made them."

"What can I do?"

"You can help me scrape the onions and the potatoes for the latkes tomorrow, and you can read about the meaning of Chanukah," Mother said, pointing to the sheets from the temple. "Then we can talk about it."

The next morning I buy a new shaving brush for my father at the corner drugstore and a pink nail polish I like for my mother. I didn't think she'd mind if I use it just in case I'm invited to a New Year's Eve party.

Peanut butter and jelly sandwich in one hand, I plop down at the kitchen table and look over the handouts. Under the heading, "Chanukah," are questions.

What does Chanukah mean?

"It's a Jewish holiday that lasts eight days honoring the rededication of the temple in Jerusalem by the Maccabees (Jewish leaders and rulers) following their victory over the Syrians in 165 BCE (before the Christian era) who wanted them to stop worshipping their God."

Why do we celebrate it for eight days?

"The small cruse (container) of oil provided light for eight days in the menorah, the candelabrum. It is considered a miracle because there was only enough oil for one day."

This happened so long ago. The Syrians were tyrants, *tyrannical.* We had Hitler. Will there always be tyrants?

In the evening, I grate the onions for the latkes taking turns with my mother. We're both crying. The onions make our eyes tear, but I think we're also crying for all those lost in Europe. I know I am. "Mother," I ask, "how come we never talk about the war?"

37

"We don't like to talk about such frightening events with our children."

We light the candles following the instructions: Place the candles in the menorah from right to left, but light them from left to right. The center candle is called the *shamash*. It's lit each night and used to light the other candles.

We read aloud the blessing over the candles: "*Baruch Atah, Adonai Elohenu, Melech haolim, asher kideshanu bemitzvotav lehadlik ner shel Chanukah*," trying our best to pronounce the words, as we don't speak or read Hebrew.

Then I read what the blessing means in English: "Blessed are you, O Lord our God, Ruler of the world, who has sanctified us through your mitzvoth (moral conduct) and commanded us to kindle the Chanukah lights."

Tonight we light them all at once because Chanukah was over last week. My father doesn't want me to light the candles. "You'll burn yourself," he says. He wants to light them himself.

"Don't be so tyrannical!" I exclaim. "I'll be careful." I strike a safety match and light the Shamash candle first, then the others, but I let my father light the last one.

The pancakes are crisp and delicious, and we have them with applesauce on the side. After dinner, my mother gives me my Chanukah present, a Bobbie bra, size AAA, my first bra!

Thinking about our tiny Christmas tree, the presents, the Christmas music, the ice-skating rink at Rockefeller Center, and how much fun we had most of that day, I ask my parents, "This doesn't mean we can't celebrate Christmas too?" My parents smile. "Of course we can." But I wonder if it's right for us to celebrate Christmas. I know my father is not Jewish, but because my mother is, under Jewish law I'm Jewish. But Christmas is so wonderful.

"What would Grandma Rachael think of us celebrating Christmas?"

"I'm not sure." She hesitates, "She may not mind. She wanted everything to be modern. Maybe she'd understand. In Canada we only celebrated Chanukah—recited the prayers, lit the candles, and ate latkes for dinner, no presents. I really don't know." She wraps her arms around me. "But I do know Grandma Rachael would be proud of you for reminding us to light the Chanukah candles."

I move into my parents' bedroom to look at Grandma Rachael's photograph. "I do love Christmas, Bing Crosby singing 'White Christmas,' and the tree at Rockefeller Center," I say to her, "but I promise I will always celebrate Chanukah, all eight nights, prayers too."

I think for a moment, then run back to her photo, "But, Grandma, I don't understand. If God is 'ruler of the world' why didn't he stop Hitler?" She looks straight at me, her lips turned down. She doesn't know either, I think, as I walk into the bathroom to try on my Bobbie bra.

December 28, 1949—our apartment
Dear RR:

Everything is not what it seems. I thought I did a kind thing by bringing home a stray cat. Instead, he scared us. Sometimes it's lonely being an only child, and I thought having a pet of my own would help. When the tabby was gone, I discovered that even though I wasn't forced from my home, WWII also affected me personally.

Chapter 9

A Stray Cat

My mother and I quiver on our kitchen table staring down at a tabby cat with one black ear. He hisses at us from the kitchen floor. I heard him crying as I walked home from sledding in the park this afternoon, his head peeped out from under a car parked on our block. I bent down and plucked him out. The cat was shivering, so I wrapped him in my new red wool scarf and carted him home. He probably had wandered away from the woods where cats and their litter hang out. He lapped up most of the milk I had poured into a cereal bowl. There's a spot of milk on his rust-colored nose. My scarf, which had dropped to the kitchen floor, he adopted as his bed. His purring kept me company as I did my homework on the kitchen table.

Mother shrieked when she saw the tabby in the kitchen. He started hissing at us, growling from somewhere deep in his throat. When he arched his back and displayed his fangs we scrambled up on the table. "What possessed you to bring this dirty, unfriendly cat home?" Mother asks. "He can leap up and scratch or bite us."

"You must have frightened him when you screamed. He was purring just before."

Fortunately, the tabby is back at the bowl lapping up the rest of the milk. He seems to have forgotten us. We climb down from the table as quietly as we can, tiptoe out of the kitchen, and close the door.

"It's cold out. I couldn't leave him out there to freeze. It was an *altruistic* thing to do." The cat scratches the bottom of the kitchen door and cries. "He sounds so lonely, like me sometimes. Can't I keep him?"

"This apartment is too small. Where could we put a litter box?" We both look around.

"Under the sink?" But I know that's not a good place.

"He might have fleas, and a veterinarian is expensive. Besides, your father would never allow it," Mother says. "He's going to be home any minute now."

"When do you feel lonely, Ruthie?" Mother asks me as we sit on the couch. "You have plenty of friends."

"Even when I'm with my friends sometimes because I'm jealous of them, except for Gaby, who doesn't have a sister."

"So you would have liked a sister?"

I nod. "You have sisters. Look how much you love them. I guess a brother would be okay too, but I'd prefer a sister."

"So why ..."

"didn't I have another child?" Mother says, completing my sentence. I nod again, trying to ignore the whimpering sounds coming from the kitchen. "It had to do with the war. We had planned on having another child ... and ..." My mother looks away from me. When she turns back I see tears in her eyes. "We wanted you to have a brother or sister. It was 1944, and we thought the war would be over shortly after D-Day, but it continued. Older men were getting draft notices. Your father received his."

"I don't understand," I say. "You had family."

"I couldn't work—you were only seven—and none of the family lived close enough to take care of you."

"Aunt Mary?"

"Freddie wouldn't give her enough money." My mother turns her head again. "So I had an ... so we decided to wait until after the war even though it turned out your father was never drafted. Then somehow it seemed too late. We just didn't think of you being lonely, not with all your aunts, uncles, and cousin Lois."

My father comes home, wrapped in the cold air from outside. "Why is the kitchen door closed?" he asks. The tabby lets out a high-pitched mew. Dad drops the mail on the black table and, without taking off his coat, throws open the kitchen door. The cat hisses as he slams the door. He glares at me.

"Well, now you know why the door is closed," I say under my breath.

"Don't mumble, Ruth. What's that dirty alley cat doing in our kitchen?"

"We didn't want the cat to leave the kitchen." I try to tell him why I brought the tabby home, avoiding his eyes burning holes into me right now. "I was just altruistic, Dad. You always tell me to be kind."

"*How could you bring a stray cat into our home? He probably has fleas. He's too old to house train, and right now he's hissing at me,*" he shouts.

"Ruthie felt sorry for the cat, Joe. He was shivering under a car near the building. Sometimes she's lonely without a brother or a sister," Mother says. My father puts his arms around my mother—something he doesn't do often, at least in front of me. He has stopped glaring at me. Instead he looks down at the floor. "She thought it would be nice to have a pet to keep her company." He nods at her, still not looking at me. "Ruthie, I guess you thought you were being kind."

Dad sneaks into the kitchen, closes the door behind him, then reappears holding the cat by the scruff of his neck. The tabby has gone slack—straight as a fishing pole. Cat hairs cling to my father's overcoat.

"This apartment is too small for a cat, even a kitten, and I'm not eating with a litter box in the kitchen. I'm taking him back to the woods." The cat still hasn't moved. "These alley cats know how to survive."

Survive! The word reminds me of my friends and their families, who survived because they escaped from Europe. It reminds me of Grandma Rachael, who survived because she fled Romania with her family. This alley cat is a survivor too. I wonder how strong I would be if I had to live in an alley, cold and scrounging for food.

"You're right, Dad," I admit.

"You see, Joe, Ruthie really is growing up," Mother comments.

"Well, if she's so grown-up she can wash her scarf, the bowl, and the floor very, very carefully. If she's so grown-up she should know better than to bring this dirty cat home," my father snaps.

"Aren't you hurting the cat holding him like that for so long?"

"No, I'm not. Their mothers carry them like this in their teeth."

"You sure know a lot about cats. Did you have a pet cat when you ...?"

"And look out for fleas!" he orders me as he carts the cat away. I catch the smile on his face as he leaves.

"Ruthie, there's something in the mail addressed to you," Mother tells me. She hands me an envelope. I rip it open. Poppy, one of the popular girls, has invited me to her New Year's Eve party. I jump up and down. "I'm invited to Poppy's party. I can wear my new clothes." I can't wait to call Karen.

"That's wonderful, but you'd better clean up the kitchen before your father comes home," she reminds me.

As I start to clean my scarf in the deep part of our kitchen sink, I don't think about the tabby anymore. I'm thinking about how I'm going to look in my new clothes, and the Sweetheart Pink nail polish I plan to borrow from Mother.

December 31, 1949–January 1, 1950–Poppy's apartment
Dear RR:

I thought the best thing that happened to me recently was being invited to Poppy's party until I found most of the kids boring and childish! Karen's right when she said, "What a bunch of jerks!" I've decided, RR, I don't want jerks in my life. I'd rather be alone. One of these days I'll meet a boy who really thinks about things.

Chapter 10

Poppy's Party

Karen also received an invitation to Poppy's party. So have Gaby, Nicole, and Anna. In fact, so has our entire eighth-grade class. So what! I get to wear my new clothes. If I don't smile, maybe no one will notice the metal cap protecting my chipped tooth.

"Karen," I say as we're tossing snowballs at each other in the park, "I wanted the invitation, and now I'm scared to go."

"Don't be silly. The food will be good. They're all a bunch of jerks, so who cares?"

"What about Harold Meister? I know you've got a crush on him," I tease. She throws a snowball in my face.

My father walks Karen and me to the party. Karen is sleeping over. Our parents make us wear galoshes. "I'll pick you girls up at twelve thirty," my father reminds us as he stashes our ugly boots in a paper bag.

We ring the doorbell. My heart is pounding, my palms are sweaty under my wool gloves, and I remind myself not to smile. "I'll never survive this party," I whisper. Poppy answers the door shouting, "*The tomboys are here!*" She doesn't say hello. We're escorted into Poppy's bedroom and add our coats to the pile on her canopied bed.

Karen heads right to the food. I'm too uncomfortable to be hungry, and besides I don't want any food to attach itself to my metal tooth. Most of the kids are bunched in the kitchen listening to *Our Miss Brooks* on the Philco radio. Larry, my super's son, comes over to me and explains that poor Miss Brooks is waiting for Mr. Boynton to ask her to a New Year's Eve party given by his Biology Department. It turns out he can't afford the five-dollar ticket for her. Instead, he leaves her a noisemaker and promises he will think of her at midnight twirling his noisemaker. Miss Brooks should give up on Mr. Boynton. I wouldn't hang around forever waiting for someone to marry me, and I certainly wouldn't spend New Year's Eve alone with a noisemaker for company!

I return to the living room. Poppy is annoyed at the kids listening to the radio. Anna is flirting with some older boy who doesn't go to our school. Gaby is in the kitchen, and Nicole and a bunch of girls are sitting on the couch looking at magazines. Boys are hanging in a corner cracking jokes, laughing, and punching each other.

Poppy places a 45 on her RCA phonograph. She and Harold begin to slow dance to the Orioles singing, "What Are You Doing New Year's Eve?" Anna and the boy I don't know dance too. Karen comes over to me. "What a bunch of jerks! Let's call your father to pick us up early," she whispers. I'm about to say yes when Larry asks me to dance.

"You look nice," he says.

"Christmas presents from my aunt and uncle," I tell him, smiling my metal cap smile, then quickly close my mouth.

Poppy brings out an empty Coca-Cola bottle. "Let's play 'Spin the Bottle!' Come on—everybody in a circle on the floor."

When we're all sitting on the floor she asks, "Who'll start the spin?"

"I will," pipes up Anna.

"If the bottle points to a boy you have to kiss him; if it points to a girl you have to spin again until it lands on a boy." Anna's spin points to Nicole, so she spins again, and it points to the boy I don't know. She struts over and gives him a long kiss on the lips and saunters away. Karen spins the bottle so hard it flies across the room and lands at Bernard's foot. "Oh, rats," I hear her mutter under her breath as she walks over and blows Bernard a kiss. I can't blame her. He's the most disgusting boy in our class. Spittle forms in the corners of his mouth.

Then it's my turn to spin. The bottle turns to Larry, and I walk over and give him a quick kiss on the lips. He turns as red as a ripe strawberry. After a few spins it's Harold's turn.

Oddly enough, I'm not thinking of Harold. I'm looking around the room: the boys are so juvenile. The girls think mainly of boys. The best part of the evening has been listening to *Our Miss Brooks* and getting dressed up in my new clothes.

Do I want to be like my classmates? Am I feeling this way because I'm shy? I wonder how the tabby cat is doing in the woods. I had forgotten all about him. I wonder if Mother is still sad that she never had another child. I wonder what would have happened if my father didn't get a draft notice. I wonder...

"Ruthie, wake up! Harold's bottle has spun to you," Gaby shouts. Harold walks over to me, smiles, and kisses me softly on the lips.

All the girls shriek, "You lucky girl! I wish it were me." I look at Harold, who is bowing, brushing away some hair that has fallen into his face. Does he think he's a matador admired by the crowd? Without thinking I remark to the group,

"What's the big deal? Harold's just one of the boys in my class. One of the more conceited ones!" And at that moment I mean just that. Harold hurries away. The rest of the bottle spinners seem stunned.

Keeping my back as straight as a dancer, I wander over to the dessert table where fudge and cookies have been set out to celebrate the new year. Not worrying that some of it might cling to my tooth, I bite into a piece of chewy chocolate fudge. Poppy's parents turn on the radio, and we all gather around it. It's almost midnight. She and her mother put glasses of fruit punch on a tray and serve them to us. Her father hands out noisemakers. The boys crank them up as loud as they can and try to hit each other with them.

"Stop making noise. We won't be able to hear!" the girls yell at them. "The ball is going to drop in one minute."

The Paramount Building clock strikes midnight. "The ball of light is descending," shouts the announcer on top of the New York Times Building. We hear the screams of New Yorkers who have been shivering in the cold for hours in Times Square waiting for this moment. "Happy New Year!" The announcer proclaims, "Welcome 1950! Happy New Year to all of you."

We hold up our glasses and toast 1950, our last year at PS 187. Next year will be different for all of us. This is my first New Year's at a party. Larry liked my skirt and blouse and asked me to dance. Harold kissed me, and it didn't mean a thing. I don't feel as scared as I did when we rang the doorbell at the beginning of the evening, but I'll be glad to leave. I *survived* the party.

Karen and I gather up our coats and thank Poppy for inviting us. "It wasn't my idea, tomboys. I didn't want to invite you. My parents made me," Poppy sneers at us. Her mother overhears her.

"Poppy, you're very rude. These girls are your classmates. Go to your room now! I'll say good-bye to your guests."

"You're making me go to my room at my own New Year's Eve party?"

"You heard your mother. Go to your room," Poppy's father orders her in front of all the kids. Poppy slumps to her room.

My father is waiting for us in the lobby. "Thank goodness that's over," Karen tells me. "What a bunch of jerks," she says as we pull up our boots.

"Do you think the tabby cat is all right out in the cold?" I ask Dad.

"Of course he is. He'll make out just fine." Karen and I start throwing snowballs at each other, and my father joins in. Karen shows me the fudge she has wrapped in napkins. The year 1950 is printed in large gold letters on the napkins. One is picked up by the breeze and floats toward the street lamp. I shout out, "Nineteen fifty is going to be a very good year!"

February 8, 1950—my apartment
Dear RR:

An ordinary afternoon with my friends made me realize I take some things for granted. I thought having a large, sunny apartment is important, but it isn't. Having Mother is. My friends saw how lucky I am. And now I do too.

Chapter 11

Hoovers and Mallomars

Looking at the drugstore calendar, thumbtacked to the kitchen wall above the telephone, I realize how much happened in December—the Chanukah blowup, the stray cat I rescued, and Poppy's New Year's Eve party. January slipped by with nothing much to write about. Now it's February. My friends are coming over this afternoon, and, as usual, I'm ashamed of our apartment.

For years, I've been asking my father if we're ever going to move to the sunny apartment on Chittenden Avenue he took us to see. He had picked out the apartment we live in without my mother seeing it, and he knows how much she hates it. So do I.

The new apartment had two bedrooms and two baths, with a large kitchen in which there was a built-in breakfast nook. I pictured my friends and I gabbing on the green, high-backed benches, our snacks on the table in the middle. My father said he would put a deposit on the apartment, and we would move there shortly.

I'd have my own room! I thought of what Aunt Mary said to my father. "Joe, she's too old to sleep in the living room." My father looked down at the floor when she spoke. "A young lady needs her privacy," she scolded him, a gold charm bracelet jingling from her wrist.

"Soon," my father says each time I ask when we're moving to the new apartment. "Don't keep asking me!" he says, his lips pursed. He taught me how to ride my bike on the steep hill on Chittenden. I remember how he planted me on my new two-wheeler and just let go of the handlebars. "Pedal slowly, then brake hard when you get to the bottom of the hill," he instructed. I fell off the bike and chipped my front tooth. "Try again," my father said. I tried until I learned to ride. Has he tried hard enough to get us that apartment? I don't ask him anymore.

My eleventh birthday passed, then my twelfth, and still no move. "I shouldn't have given Joe the deposit money," I overheard Aunt Mary tell my mother in the kitchen. I've heard my other aunts say often, "Money just burns a hole in Joe's pocket." When I was little, I looked for burn holes in his pockets. Now I understand what "burning a hole in his pocket" means. It means that my father spends without thinking. It means that my father no longer has the deposit money. I'm glad I didn't tell my friends we were moving. At least I don't have to make lame excuses to them as he does to me.

I figure I won't move out of here until I finish college, get a job, and save enough money to rent my own place. I plan to live in Greenwich Village, where all the writers and artists live. I won't be able to afford a large apartment at first, so it's a good thing I'm used to this one.

Since it's my turn to have my friends over, I especially think about how nice it would be to live in the Chittenden apartment. At least I can spruce up this one. When I put on Mother's frilly apron, I'm the pretty lady in the Hoover vacuum cleaner ad in *Ladies Home Journal*. *Obsessed* with tidying and cleaning, I Hoover the living room carpet and Bon Ami the bathroom. Mother's bra, girdle, and stockings, drip-drying on the foldout clothes rack, are temporarily stowed in the clothes hamper.

In the living room, I half-open the venetian blinds to let in the dim light from the alley and to shutter our neighbor's apartment directly opposite ours. I pick up my father's *Field & Stream* magazines. In the hall closet, his polished fishing rods greet me like soldiers at attention while I search for hangers for my friends' coats. His gas mask, left over from his air-raid warden's duties during the war, stares down at me from the top shelf.

I spent some of my allowance on yellow roses I place in a vase on the black leather table. The chipped chrome kitchen table I cover with a new yellow-and-white-check tablecloth. Mallomar cookies, Cheetos, and potato chips are in dishes on the kitchen table.

I'm *obsessed* with Mallomar cookies. They're shaped like a bell, but Anna calls them Mallo-breasts. Dark chocolate covers a marshmallow filling on top of a graham cracker-like crust. Of course I eat one as I wait for my friends. Mallomar heaven!

The apartment is as good as it's going to get. It will never be the apartment where my friends and I could snack in the breakfast nook. So what if it isn't? It's selfish to complain about not moving. Look what grandmother and my friends went through! Yet, I'm still disappointed. I'm ashamed of our apartment when they come over. I wish I didn't feel that way, but I do.

I hear them clomp down the hall. When we're all squeezed around the kitchen table eating Mallomars and drinking glasses of milk, Anna says, "Isn't this the most delicious cookie? It looks just like a breast."

"Maybe I can stuff them in my Bobbie bra," I quip.

Anna rolls her eyes. She licks off the chocolate topping slowly. "Your mom leaves the best snacks," she says, chocolate smeared over her lips. "I had fun at Poppy's party. I love playing 'Spin the Bottle.'"

"We noticed," we all chime in.

"When Harold's bottle swung to you, and he kissed you, I was so jealous," Nicole said.

"I couldn't believe you said out loud how conceited Harold is. Even if it's true," Anna added.

"It just popped out of my mouth. But I meant it. Besides Karen and I weren't really invited. Poppy's mother forced her to ask us. I don't care anymore."

Gabby sees I'm uncomfortable and changes the subject.

"No, don't change the subject yet," I tell Gaby. "All of you in a way made me look at things differently."

"It was the poems we wrote in my house," Gaby said. I nod.

"I don't want to think about such sad things ever again," Anna says. "Tell us about the alley cat you brought home. Did he have fleas? Did your father have a fit? My mother would." I tell them how scared we were and how my father picked the cat up by the scruff of his neck to bring him to the alley.

"The cat we had to leave in France didn't have fleas. Puff was very affectionate. My mother shooed her off, but she slept at the foot of my bed anyway," Nicole says quietly.

My friends are silent for a while. I want to tell them about the conversation with my mother, but I don't. I don't tell them I nearly had a brother or sister; that I suspect Mother somehow stopped her pregnancy because my father received his draft notice. Anna probably would remark, "I bet your mother had an abort …" I don't want to hear that word, even though it's probably true.

"I just love your mother. She's the sweetest woman," Nicole remarks, as we march off to the living room. "My mother says that your mom is such a lady." I didn't ask her what Mrs. Girard thinks about my dad. I knew the answer.

"Your apartment is cozy, not like mine. I hate our long, dark halls, and we can't seem to get rid of roaches in the kitchen," Gaby grimaces.

I never think our apartment is cozy, but maybe it is. I think of Nicole's mother, who fusses over her but is very cold, or Gaby's mother, who is kind to everyone, but often seems unhappy.

About to start my homework on the kitchen table I've cleared of snacks, one Mallomar cookie is left. I slowly lick the chocolate off the cookie the way Anna does. Chocolate dribbles on my blouse. I know Mother won't be angry over the mess I make as I try to rub the stain out with a dishcloth.

Tonight we're having baby lamb chops for dinner. That makes me think of all the wonderful meals Mother prepares in this little kitchen. So we don't have a cozy nook with built-in benches! I smile a chocolate smile as I wait for her to come home from work.

March 30, 1950—PS 187
Dear RR:

I try so hard in Mrs. Stepp's math and sewing classes, but it doesn't help. I don't know if I'm a dumb math student, or I'm so scared in her class I can't think. I'm just as bad in her sewing class. Mrs. Stepp makes me feels incapable. What an insensate teacher she is, the opposite of my English teacher! My life can be hard sometimes. I know Jews were not allowed to attend many of the schools in Europe during the war. But reminding myself of much harder lives doesn't always make me feel better—just guilty. I wonder what kind of a teacher Mrs. Stepp would have been in Europe. Would she have picked on Jews?

Chapter 12

Old Squeaky

I never raise my hand in Mrs. Stepp's class. Not even if I have to go to the bathroom in the worst way. I'm so frightened I feel I'm going to vomit when she calls me to the blackboard for a math problem. She may want me to demonstrate *how* I solve the problem. Even if I puzzled out how to solve the problem on my homework sheet, when I have to work it out in front of Mrs. Stepp, I forget.

Today I fold into my desk, hoping the scarred wood top will hide me from her roving eye. When she snakes around the classroom, her space shoes squeak. The class has nicknamed her "The Squeaks" or "Old Squeaky." Would I like to see her come into class one day with her slip hanging below her skirt or, better yet, have her pass a real loud smelly one (like Albert), when she's up at the blackboard.

"Ruth, come up to the blackboard and solve this problem!" I hope it's not a word problem. The worst for me are the word problems where the trains are going in different directions at different speeds, and I have to figure the times and distances it takes them to travel somewhere. Trust me, I will never be a trainman.

I am a miserable math pupil; miserable because I stink at arithmetic and miserable because I'm in Mrs. S's class. I'm also miserable when my father helps me with my math homework.

I've been taught a different math than when my father went to school one hundred years ago. Also, my father has an Italian accent and speaks in incomplete sentences. For example, he'll say, "You take the 'whatchamacallit' and move it to the right and then ..." his voice trails off as he mumbles the end of the sentence. When I ask him what he means, he usually ends up getting angry and walking out of the apartment, and I end up asking my mother, "Why did you marry him?"

"Ruth, stop daydreaming and go up to the blackboard! How often do I have to ask you?" Mrs. S demands.

Up I go. As if I have a choice. I'm a little encouraged because I know how to do the division problems on the board, but that doesn't stop my knees from shaking and perspiration from running down my armpits. I produce the right answer and scurry back to my seat. I'm so happy, and a bit proud of myself, but then I hear The Squeaks scream at me, *"Ruth, did I tell you to leave? Go back to the board. I'm going to give you some fractions to do."*

I look at the problem Mrs. S has scribbled, and I get so rattled I can't understand the problem. I write down the wrong answer. *"Ruth, it's clear you didn't do your homework. Anyone can learn fractions! Go back to your seat!"*

I don't tell Mrs. S that I did the homework but still don't understand fractions or that her yelling at me in front of the class doesn't help. Everyone is staring at me as I slink back to my seat trying not to look at anyone, not even Karen. Of course The Squeaks will make me stay after school with the rest of the dumb math kids for extra help from Bernard, the most unpopular student in the class.

To make matters worse, today I have my sewing class, also taught by the *insensate* Mrs. Stepp. I cannot sew. I evolve from a long line of nonsewers. The females in my family are great cooks, but there's not a sewer among them.

In class we're beginning to make our graduation dresses. Six new electric Singer sewing machines take over the classroom. Mrs. Stepp is so excited that I'm waiting for her to launch them with bottles of champagne. The two old-fashioned pedal machines operated by foot have been shoved into the back.

Last Thursday, the day the new machines arrived, I jammed one of them ... broke is probably more accurate. We were practicing on leftover pieces of fabric to acquaint ourselves with using the new machines. I did something wrong with the bobbin. It fed the needle too much thread and broke the needle in half. Mrs. Stepp placed her hands firmly on my shoulders and yanked me out of my chair. "*You are banished forever from using an electric sewing machine,*" she sputtered.

Anyway, here I am today unevenly sewing a hemline of dotted Swiss material on the foot-pedal machine, which I prefer to the electric one anyhow. Its wooden top and black scroll sides and foot pedal are much more elegant than the new sewing machines. Mrs. S shrieks out, "*Ruth, you owe the school one dollar for the needle you broke last week. Did you forget to ask your father for the money?*" I try to ignore the snickering from the girls who can sew straight hems on the electric machines without breaking the needle.

I'm afraid to ask my father for one dollar for a new needle. I'll ask Mother for the money. I shudder to think of his reaction if the school has to hire a repairman to fix the machine. We'll have to pay for that, too.

I adore my next class, English. English and creative writing are my favorite subjects. Miss Devaney teaches these. She encourages everyone, even Sophie Chengarian, who is a little slow. Mrs. Devaney's hair is tied back in a bun. She wears high-necked dresses and is unmarried. People call her an *old maid.* Mrs. Stepp is the *old maid,* so dried up and cold. Miss

Devaney is warm and caring, even though she's strict. I raise my hand in her class.

In English we write in a black-and-white-speckled hardcover notebook with lined paper. Our homework every day is to rewrite the day's work, spelling words, or grammar rules, and the next day Miss Devaney checks our notebooks. We use a ruler to make one and one half-inch margins on each side of the page. If we have an inkblot or a word crossed out, we have to redo the page. It sounds boring, but I've learned how to write, spell, and check my work because of all the rewriting. In the back of our notebooks we list new vocabulary words and their meanings. Since September I've learned and used about thirty new vocabulary words.

Today, Miss Devaney makes an announcement: "Class, the *Daily Mirror* is having a citywide contest." She writes the topic on the blackboard.

"What It Means to Be an American."

400-500 words Deadline: July 5

She continues, "First prize is an apprentice job at the paper over Labor Day weekend, September second, third, and fourth. The sign-up sheet is on my desk."

I'll write about Grandma Rachael—how hard it must have been for her and her family to be forced to leave Romania and how frightening it must have been to resettle in Canada, and later in America. I'll write about my father, who emigrated from Italy with his father and stepfamily when he was just three. I'll write about my friends and their families, who had fled Europe because of Hitler. I push past Bernard, so I'm the first one to sign.

Bernard reminded me of math detention. At least after that, I've something to look forward to. I'm going to see the musical *On the Town* with Mother, and I can tell her about the contest. I'm not worried about bumping into Old Squeaky at the movie theater. We're seeing a musical, not a horror movie.

March 30, 1950, 11:00 p.m.–Mount Sinai Hospital

Dear RR:

I look forward to movie night with Mother. Everything about it makes me happy. Walking past the shops on our way, hot dogs at the deli, talking together, and seeing a movie. And now, instead of climbing into bed, I'm in the hospital with blood on my clothes while my father and I wait to hear from the doctor. I'm so glad I have you with me, RR, because writing is the only thing I can do to keep me from screaming. Life is filled with both sadness and happiness. I had both the same day.

Chapter 13

A Night at the Movies

The house painters attempted to paint the kitchen last week, but my father threw them out. When I say threw out, I'm not exaggerating. He shouted at the painters as they stood in the hallway with their buckets of paint, "*Stupes, where'd you learn to paint? You don't prep the walls. You slap the paint on. Tell the super I'll paint the apartment!*" The painters grabbed the rest of their stuff and bolted. The last time he also threw out the painters. You'd think they would learn and not come back again. I was mortified when our neighbors opened their doors because of my father's yelling!

After I come home from detention, I try to avoid my father, who's prepping the walls of our kitchen in his painter's clothes—white-paint-streaked overalls, painter's cap, and old shoes splattered with paint. It's never calm to be around my father, but it's really dreadful to be near him when he paints. It's a given he'll find something I've done wrong. Last time I tripped on a drop cloth and planted my foot in some paint, which rubbed off on the living room carpet. I skirt the drop cloths on my way into the bedroom, where I say hello to Grandma Rachael's photograph.

When Mother comes home I tell her I hope I haven't broken the new electric sewing machine, that I did break the sewing needle, and that I owe the school one dollar.

Mother gives me the money for the needle and warns me not to say anything to my father unless I have to. "It could be that thread was tangled around the bobbin, and the school handyman can repair the sewing machine."

We'll walk to the delicatessen for an early dinner before the movie. I practically skip to the elevator because I've avoided my father. I'll spend the evening alone with Mother, doing our favorite thing—going to a movie. And I've finished after-school detention, where I was fraction-tortured by *goodie-goodie* Bernard, who planted a sloppy wet kiss on my cheek as I dashed out the door.

We come upon Mrs. Green in the lobby. Does she live there and wait for me?

"It's good for you two to go out tonight when that man is painting!" she says to us, her mole hair waving back and forth. Does everyone in the building know my father is painting our apartment?

I ignore Mrs. Green, and Mother nods politely. Thursday night is too special to let Mrs. Green bother us. We'll see Frank Sinatra, Gene Kelly, and Ann Miller. Mother worships movie stars. She calls the stars by their first names, as if she knows them personally. She'll say "Joan" was wonderful in *Mildred Pierce*, meaning Joan Crawford.

We walk down the hill to 181st Street, then Broadway, passing the RKO movie theatre, and a little later the five-and-ten-cent store. We're singing "Mairzy Doats." Mother has a lovely voice. She sings on tune and knows the lyrics to popular songs.

> Mairzydoats
> Andoesedotes
> Andl'illambseativy
> Akid'leativytoo
> Wouldn't you?

I sing along very softly, combining the words like the popular singers. I'm one of the kids told to mouth words when we sing in a school assembly. My father and I can't carry a tune.

Entering the delicatessen, we choose a table against the wall. The waiter knows us and asks, "The usual?" We nod. He doesn't smile. Do waiters in Jewish delicatessens get fired if they look happy? He plunks down our hot dogs with sauerkraut, French fries, and cream soda.

"Mother, I don't look or act like the popular girls in my class," I blurt out. "I was only invited to Poppy's party because her parents made her, and everyone there was a bunch of jerks, so I don't know why I care."

"Oh, Ruthie," she says, resting her hand on mine.

"But I want to look like the other girls." My eyes well up.

"I know how you feel. I wasn't popular either. I didn't look like the other girls because of the pimples on my face. That's when I started to like movies. I wanted to disappear inside the movie."

I look at Mother. Her skin is flawless now. Her hair, parted on the side, is dark brown and wavy. Her nose is prominent but not as large as my father's. I think it makes her look regal. There's hope for me yet. Mother's the kindest person I know. She listens to me and makes me feel loved.

"Perhaps it's time to wear a light-color lipstick and a skirt once in a while outside of school," Mother suggests.

"It's not fair. Boys wear pants all the time, and we have to wear dumb ..." I don't complete the sentence because I know she is right.

"Soon you'll have a new cap on your front tooth, and you have such a pretty smile." I full smile at her compliment. "Just be yourself. You're growing up slower than the other girls. But you'll see. High school will be different."

I look down at the pants I changed into after school, then Mother's pretty red print dress that swishes when she walks, and the white gloves she wears when she goes out. I didn't bother to change the white blouse I wore to school, the one I notice has a smudge of ketchup. I'm hoping the ketchup streak looks like blood. I'd rather cut myself than look like a slob. Reaching into my bag to get a hanky, I see my diary, which I took to school today. My father paints the insides of our closets, and I didn't want him to find it. I hope he'll cover Grandma's photograph.

That makes me think about her. I would like to ask Mother why Grandma looks so sad in her photo. But not tonight! We may not have as many Thursday nights together when I'm in high school. I don't want to ruin this time—this time of sitting in the deli, and this time of the two of us going to the movies together.

"I signed up for a writing contest sponsored by the *Daily Mirror*. The topic is "What It Means to Be an American.""

"You could write about your grandmother and your friends."

"That's just what I'm going to write about, Dad, too. And maybe you can tell me more about Grandma."

Mother has a funny look on her face. She says, "You'll write a wonderful essay," but doesn't say more about her mother. I wonder why.

At the movie theater, we enter through the ornate Indochinese decorations. The theater can seat thousands of people. A wide carpeted marble staircase in the center of the foyer leads to the loge and bathrooms. The ceiling above the staircase is designed to look like the *aurora borealis*—a stairway to the stars! Each time I walk up this *stairway to the stars* to use the bathroom, I pretend I'm a glamorous movie star.

"Mother, this theater is so sumptuous." Because it's a school night, we're only going to see the main feature. On Saturday afternoons my friends and I see a double feature, coming attractions, a newsreel, a cartoon, and a continuing serial.

As we leave the theater smiling, we say at the same time, "Wasn't that movie wonderful?" My father has given us money to take a cab home because he doesn't want us to walk alone at night. Mother hails a cab. Sitting in the backseat, we sing,

New York, New York,
It's a wonderful town.
The Bronx is up
And the Battery's down
The ...

The taxi screeches to a halt. I hear a thud and the sound of metal crashing into metal. We scream and topple forward. I turn to my mother, crying, "Are you okay?" She brings her hands to her forehead and nose and bleeds onto her white gloves. I reach over to try to hold her, but she slumps over on the seat.

The cabdriver paces outside his damaged cab. His front fender is crumpled on the street. He curses at the driver of the car who stopped short in front of him. A large crowd gathers around the two men. No one checks on us. No one looks in the back of the cab. I must get help. I push open the door on my side and run out, screaming, "My mother is hurt. Someone get help! We need help!"

A woman looking out her first-floor window yells out to me, "I'll call for an ambulance."

"Please call my father, too, LO. 8-1324." Somehow saying our telephone number makes me feel in control.

I dash into the backseat. I see a metal plate with the driver's name and license number smeared with blood. That is what

Mother must have hit. Blood covers the back seat and Mother's pretty dress. I lift her gently off the seat and hold her head in my lap. By the time my father reaches us the ambulance and the police have arrived, sirens clearing their way. Sweating and out of breath, my father must have run all the way from our apartment about twelve blocks away. Pushing me aside in the cab, he cradles my mother's head in his arms, tucking her dress around her to keep her warm. He's crying.

We climb into the back of the ambulance alongside Mother, who has been placed on a gurney. The sirens clear a path once more as we're whisked away to the hospital. When the attendant in the ambulance cleans the blood from my mother's head wounds, I want to fold into my father's arms, but he hasn't let go of my mother's hand since we entered the ambulance. The attendant checks me too because my shirt is stained with blood. I tell him I'm all right, at least on the outside. Inside, my stomach is churning.

At the hospital, we pace in the waiting room, keeping an eye out for the doctor. My father's paint-stained clothes and shoes stand out. White paint has dribbled over parts of his eyebrows and part of his mustache. I'm embarrassed by how he looks and angry with myself for feeling that way when my mother was just in an accident.

I wander into the hospital chapel. Dad follows me.

"I want to light a candle for Mother."

"Jewish girls don't light candles."

"But you can light a candle."

"I don't light candles anymore, but I will tonight." We hold a candle together and light it. We walk back to the waiting room, where we stare at the swinging doors.

Finally, the doctor emerges. Mother has sustained a mild concussion and a broken nose, but she'll be fine, although she's to remain in the hospital for a few days for observation. My father starts to cry again. I can barely move my legs. We take a cab home. Picturing the blood on the seat in the cab in which we had our accident, I sit on the floor. Dad must feel better because he's sitting in front with the cabdriver, telling him all the people he's going to sue. I cover my ears.

At home, he calls Aunt Mary. She'll arrange for a housekeeper to do the cleaning and cooking in our apartment for a few weeks. That will allow my mother some time to rest when she gets home. My father calls Sollie and asks him for the name of a lawyer. He doesn't try to comfort me. Is it because I'm almost thirteen, old enough to take care of myself? But I do need comforting tonight. I need my mother to hold me and tell me she's fine. I can't imagine a world without my mother in it. My friends are right—she is the dearest person.

I want to sleep. I'm exhausted, but when I close my eyes I see Mother's blood on her white gloves. I hear the thud when her head hit the metal plate. I hear the sound of steel crashing into steel. I see my mother pass out. I hear the cabdriver, the other driver, and the people on the street argue about who's at fault, ignoring my mother and me. I think of the woman who called an ambulance and then my father. I never thanked her. My white blouse, once stained only with ketchup, is now stained with blood.

Mother will be fine, the doctor said. *My mother will be fine!* But she's still in the hospital. While Dad's in the shower, I walk into the bedroom to speak to Grandma's photo. "Please watch over your daughter tonight."

The doctor said she would be coming home in a few days. I'll buy her some flowers with my allowance money. A piece of Milk Duds is caught in my back molar. I'm too tired to brush my teeth. I try to sing myself to sleep.

Mairzydoats

Andoesedotes ...

What a childish song, I think as I feel myself drifting off.

April 21, 1950—my apartment

Dear RR:

Tonight my cousin Lois revealed a shocking secret about Grandma Rachael. She also told me about Doris, Lois's sister, whom I didn't know existed. Lois is sleeping in the living room. I'm in the bedroom, sitting on my parents' bed. Writing to you, RR, calms me the way it did after the cab accident. I look up at Grandma's Rachael's photo on the dresser. It's been the best birthday of my life, Grandma, because Lois gave me something that belonged to you. "Look what I've fastened to my pajamas. It's beating next to my heart. PS: Thank you for watching after your daughter. She's fine—just the way the doctor said she would be."

Chapter 14

My Grandmother's Photo

I'll be thirteen in one week! A teenager finally! I'm hoping that I, along with the spring flowers, will start to bloom. Breasts would be a good start, and to have a boy other than Larry notice I'm alive would be moving in the right direction.

My cousin Lois is sleeping over tonight to celebrate my birthday. My parents are playing gin rummy with neighbors, so Lois and I will be alone. I can't wait to question her about boys and sex!

We have to celebrate before my birthday because Lois, who everyone says looks like Elizabeth Taylor, was married last week! She and her new husband are moving to New Mexico, far away from me. The phone rings, and I run to answer it in my parents' bedroom.

"How's your mother?" Lois asks. I tell her she's even gone back to work. "I'll be over a little early, in about an hour," Lois says. I ask her why. "There's a lot to talk about. I want to tell you some things about Grandma," she replies, "things I don't want to tell you on the phone. Oh, and I have a special present for you."

A special present! And what's she going to tell me about our grandmother? I glance over at Grandma Rachael's photograph framed by other family photos on top of the white faux French dresser. This is our only picture of her. When I look into her eyes I feel she sees me. I want to walk through the picture's glass keeping us apart. I want to feel her ample body hug me. I wonder what she was thinking?

I'm named after her, although I would have preferred Rachael to Ruth. Ruth is a *derivative* of Rachael. My eyebrows and eyes are shaped like hers—thick eyebrows and large wide-set eyes. I wonder about the color of her eyes and hair because the photograph is not in color. Her dark hair is pulled into in an upsweep, stretched over a rat and parted in the middle. A white, collarless blouse shows off an embroidered jumper. What leaps out at me is a watch dangling from a brooch covered with jewels and pinned to her clothing. That's just about where the photo ends.

I don't know why I stare at Grandma's photo so often. I just do. Some days I imagine her sitting in the kitchen with Mother, having a cup of coffee, whispering secrets. I wish my grandmother could be with Lois and me tonight.

I snatch Grandma's photo from its home on my parents' dresser. I have already made up the sofa bed in the living room with fresh sheets, and I prop Grandma's photograph on the back of our pillows.

"Grandma," I say to the photo, "I think I know why you look sad. You've had a hard life." I didn't know yet how hard.

I know my grandparents were forced to leave a city named Iasi in Romania near the Russian border because of the pogroms. The army killed civilians, mainly Jews. Did my family leave Europe "just in time," as my friends' families did, except in an earlier time?

I also know that my grandparents had two young sons who died in Romania, but a boy and three girls survived, and in 1908 the remaining family immigrated to Canada, where Mother was born.

I study Grandma's photograph. I think it was taken when she was in her early fifties. I know she was sixteen when she had her first child. I couldn't imagine being a mother at sixteen, but it was different in her time. How I wish I could really talk to her. There are so many things I would ask. I'm still staring at her photo when the doorbell rings.

Lois and I hug in the hallway inside my apartment. She places a small box wrapped in shiny yellow paper on the black table. "A surprise for your birthday," she tells me. What could it be?

As soon as Lois gets settled she changes into her pajamas. I'm already wearing my baby doll pajamas. Mother's rolled cookies, filled with jam and walnuts, still warm from the oven, fill the kitchen with their aroma. We bring the cookies into the living room, place them on the end table next to the clock, and sit cross-legged on the bed. "I've made Grandma part of our pajama party."

"She is the pajama party," Lois says.

Before I can ask her what she means by such an odd remark, she asks me about school and my friends. "What couldn't you tell me on the phone about Grandma, and what do you mean she is the pajama party?"

Lois takes the photo into her hands. "My mother told me she had brown eyes and brown hair, like you."

I nod. I wish she'd get to the point. "I think you're now old enough to know ... some things our parents won't talk about ... like ..."

Now I know we're not going to talk about sex or boys. I don't care about that anymore. I want to know what she's going to tell me. There must be stories I haven't been told.

"Ruthie, you're having an important birthday next week. You're old enough to know about Grandma Rachael."

"More than about the pogroms? And about her two sons?" Lois nods.

"I know about the fire that burned down the boarding house she ran in Montreal!"

"More than that!" Lois stares at Grandma's photo, pulling the blanket over her pajamas.

"Sometime after Grandpa Joseph died, Grandma started a catering business to support herself and the children," Lois begins.

"Yes, I know that," I said, wanting Lois to know that I've been told some things. "Mother also told me that Grandma used to arrange marriages for relatives who came over from Romania."

"She did." But this isn't what she wants me to know. I can tell by the way she's looking at Grandma's photo and not at me.

"I can't imagine someone choosing my husband. Suppose she chose Bernard, who plants sloppy wet kisses on the cheek of any girl unlucky enough to get near him. Yuck!"

Lois laughs and then looks grim.

"Sometime in the 1930s, the family moved to Staten Island," she explains. "Aunt Mary paid for everyone to come to America. She also rented a house. You might have been told she had followed a bandleader to New York City. Their marriage was annulled because he drank too much."

I nod.

"Was it hard for Grandma to leave Canada and start over again in America?"

"It had to be. She left cousins and friends behind."

Lois continues, "The sisters helped Aunt Mary run a dress shop she had bought, and Grandma, even though she had diabetes, ran the house." My cousin gets up and walks around the room. "This is what no one told you. No one told me until I was about your age. It's going to be hard for you to hear. It was for me." Lois takes my hands. "Medicine was pretty primitive then, not the way it is now. Often diabetics had amputations, and ..."

"No!" I don't want to hear this. I look at Grandma. The tears well up in my eyes.

"Where, Lois?"

"At the knees. Her legs were amputated at the knees."

"At the knees?" I cry out. I place my hands on my knees and imagine what it would be like not to have the rest of my legs. I couldn't ride my bike, ice-skate, dance, or even walk to school. I couldn't get to the hideout. Would I have any friends? My stomach feels like it did when I saw Mother bleeding in the taxicab.

"She used a wheelchair, but she had *coyick.*"

"*Coyick?*"

"*Coyick* means courage." What would I be like if that happened to me? Would I have courage? "Even in a wheelchair, Grandma cooked the meals and took care of little Doris."

"Doris?"

"Doris was my sister. Grandma adored her. My mother told me Doris would sit on Grandma's lap or crawl into bed with her."

"What happened to Doris? I never knew I had another cousin."

"She died of polio when she was five," Lois tells me. "She died before I was born."

"I'm so sorry, Lois!" I speak to Grandma's photo as if she's in the room with us. "I'm so sorry, Grandma."

"That's when Grandma lost her *coyick*. She just gave up," Lois says, holding back tears. "My mother told me that Grandma kept on saying that it should have been her who died, not Doris."

I run into the bathroom to get a box of tissues. Tears are running down my face—not just because of Doris's death, but because of how Grandma must have felt when her granddaughter died. I hurry back into the living room. I don't want to leave Lois alone. Back in bed, Lois and I listen to the ticking of the clock.

Lois speaks so softly I have to strain to hear her. "A few weeks after Doris's death, everyone was working at the shop ..." Lois says nothing for a while. "Grandma closed the window and door in the kitchen, lit the gas jet in the oven, placed her head inside the oven ... and ..."

We continue to stare at her photo, not looking at each other, and not speaking. "Who found her?" I ask.

Lois squeezes my hand. "Your mother!"

"Mother!" My voice seems to come from my stomach, not my throat. I don't know what to say. I can't even cry. The tears are too deep inside me. Grandma Rachael must have loved my mother so, her last child, the child who was born in Canada. Grandma must have given up on life not to think about how her death would hurt my mother and the rest of her family.

"I'm sure Grandma didn't plan to hurt your mother. Your mother just came home first. Her migraine headaches may be because she found Grandma like that," Lois suggests. "That's what the family thinks, anyway." She puts her arms around me.

I picture my mother when she has a migraine headache. She shuts down, pulls the shades in the bedroom, and remains in bed for a couple of days. My father and I shut down as well. The apartment seems so empty without my mother bustling about. Would I come home one day and find that Mother has taken too many painkillers? I nearly lost her in the cab accident.

Lois sighs again. "My mother was pregnant with me, but she never told Grandma because in those days you waited until you showed before you told anyone. Maybe if Grandma knew, she wouldn't have done what she did."

I can't stop crying. I feel so bad for my mother and for the whole family. I return Grandma's photo to the top of the dresser in my parents' bedroom. I can't look at her sad face anymore. Lois comes in and cradles me in her arms. "I made a mistake. I've told you too much. I'm sorry." She looks away from me for a minute and then runs out of the bedroom. "Here's the special present for your thirteenth birthday," she says and hands me my gift.

I rip off the shiny yellow wrapping paper. Inside a black velvet box is a watch attached to a jeweled pin, its ruby and sapphire jewels sparkling. I can't believe I'm holding the brooch watch I've stared at so often in Grandma's photo. Carefully, I lift the watch out of the box.

"My mother gave me Grandma's watch when I turned thirteen. I want you to have it now." I hold grandma's watch in my hand, the jewels twinkle up at me. I break into a smile.

"Do you know who gave Grandma this watch?"

"Grandpa."

"Please pin it to my pajamas. I want to sleep with her watch tonight," I beg her.

Lois pins the watch to my baby doll. "Wind the watch slowly. It'll run for a short while. It's very old."

"This is the best present you could have given me." I feel the watch press into my skin as I hug her tightly. "You were right to tell me everything tonight. It's time I learned all our family history."

Lois falls asleep, but I can't. I tiptoe into my parents' bedroom to look at Grandma's photograph. Grandma Rachael looks straight at me as she always does.

I think I understand what you want me to know. You ran out of time. I run my fingers over her watch. *I know that you are a part of me. I promise to carry your coyick inside me forever.*

The light from the street lamp on the block highlights Grandma's photo. I imagine the corners of her mouth turning up. I realize that my wish was granted. Grandma Rachael was at my thirteenth birthday celebration after all!

April 28, 1950—the Stork Club
Dear RR:

Aunt Mary took me to lunch today at the famous Stork Club. My friends envied me for "lunching" at the "Club" with my glamorous aunt. She is glamorous, but I don't like how my aunt lives—thinking mostly of how she looks and going to fancy places. I want to do something more significant with my life, so why do I like being envied for doing what she does?

Chapter 15

I See the Cowardly Lion

To celebrate my thirteenth birthday tomorrow, Aunt Mary is taking me to lunch this Saturday at the famous Stork Club on Fifty-Third Street in midtown Manhattan. Aunt Mary and her wealthy boyfriend, Freddie, often dine at the Stork Club, but this is my first time.

Karen has instructed me to remember all the details of the lunch, including the celebrities I see and what they're wearing and doing. I doubt I'll notice. I'll be sweating a tropical rainstorm under my armpits as I do when I'm nervous, and I'm always nervous with Aunt Mary. She's so perfect, the way she looks and speaks and dresses. I'm an ugly country mouse around her. And she always tells me to do something like wear red lipstick, or stand up straight, or not to walk with my feet turned out. I'm surprised she'll allow herself to be seen with me at *her* Stork Club.

This morning my aunt called with last-minute instructions: "Sherman may be over to say hello during lunch. Make sure you sit up straight and smile when you greet him." "Sherman" is Sherman Billingsley, the owner of the Stork Club. I saw him on the television show broadcast weekly from the club. I never thought I'd be meeting him. Now my aunt has made me even more nervous. When I smile, the metal cap on my front tooth flashes like the tinfoil lining from a stick of gum. The best I can do is half-smile for Sherman. The best I can do is never enough for Aunt Mary.

Gaby and Karen pick out clothing for me to wear. I look gawky in the outfit they choose: a black-and-white-check cast-off suit with a skirt that's too big. Gaby safety pins it smaller. At least the jacket will hide the sweat rings in the armpits of my Peter Pan collared blouse. My garter belt slips down to my belly button causing the nylons to wrinkle around my ankles. I'm five feet one and weigh ninety pounds. My family has nicknamed me "skinnymarink" after a Jimmy Durante recording of the children's song "Skinnymarink." I hate it when they call me that!

Gaby hands me our shared pair of black enamel earrings to wear. Karen sticks a hankie in the top pocket of the jacket as a finishing touch. I don't feel very finished.

Karen laughing at how I look doesn't help me feel better. She says I should wear my dungarees and fringed suede jacket instead.

"Why don't you go to the Stork Club in my place, smarty!" I snap at her.

"Are you kidding? I wouldn't be found dead in such a phony place." Karen doesn't answer when I ask why she wants to know about the celebrities I'll see there. My friends keep running to the window to see if Aunt Mary's chauffeur, Charlie, is parked downstairs.

"He's here. Give us a ride! Give us a ride!" they beg. Now I know why they helped me get dressed. I agree to let them ride with me in the Cadillac down the hill to just before the entrance to the West Side Highway.

Mrs. Green spots us. "Aren't you hoity-toity, getting a ride in your aunt's fancy black Cadillac?" she screeches when she sees us pile into the long black limousine. I admit I don't mind the attention, even from Mrs. Green. It's sumptuous to ride in such an expensive car, but I feel out of place. That's how I feel when I'm with Aunt Mary—out of place.

By the time Charlie drops me in front of the Stork Club, I'm not only sweating under my armpits, but my palms are wet, too. I wipe them with the hankie from my jacket pocket.

The entrance is under a green canopy. A tall, elegant, blue-uniformed doorman wearing a cap with gold embroidered trim greets me and slowly moves aside a gold chain to allow me to pass into the club. "That looks heavy," I comment.

"It's fourteen-karats," he says with a hint of a smile. He ushers me into a small lobby flanked by telephone booths and a checkroom. The blonde checkroom attendant eyes me up and down. The headwaiter escorts me into an L-shaped dining room mirrored to reflect the crystal chandelier. I catch a glimpse of my sagging stockings. "Your aunt Mary is expecting you," he says, leading me toward a table in the middle of the restaurant.

My aunt poses at a table covered by a white cloth, with a filter tip cigarette in one hand and a drink in the other. She wears a black crepe suit. A two-strand pearl necklace clasped by red rubies encircles her neck. Her dark hair is pulled back in a chignon at the nape of her head. A white-feathered cloche hat nests on her hair. My aunt looks elegant, as usual. My mother has an elegance of her own, I think. Not as sophisticated, but less *pretentious.*

I stand up straight and try to keep my feet from pointing out as I walk toward her. Couldn't she have picked a table in the back of the room? She sees me and blows me a kiss. Her gold charm bracelet jingles. I know better than to hug her because it will mess up her makeup and hair.

Aunt Mary notices what I'm wearing and exclaims, "Who gave you that suit? I must buy you a new suit!" Then she sees the earrings. "It's better to wear no earrings than cheap ones." I run my tongue over my capped tooth. "Well, dear," Aunt

Mary says, her look moving to my face, "at least you put on red lipstick. It brightens up your face, you know."

My aunt ends many of her sentences with "you know." She doesn't know that the "Fire and Ice" Revlon red lipstick on my lips makes me feel plain compared to Suzy Parker, the model who advertises it. The only thing she knows about me is I love creamed spinach.

I look around the club, *her* club. I see a photo of Lucille Ball and Frank Sinatra. Framed photos of other celebrities cover the back walls. A tall wooden stork decorates each tabletop. The stork sports a black top hat and a painted monocle. A small beaker of water at its feet holds one red rose. "The Stork Club" is imprinted in white letters on the rim of the black ashtray and the cover of the matchbook.

When the waiter appears, Aunt Mary orders a hamburger with a side of creamed spinach for me. She orders a salad for herself. From her monogrammed cigarette case on the table, she removes a cigarette. The monograms are MAH, which stand for Mary Ann Hill, but her real name is Maitala Fanny Itzkavitsky. She had her name changed when she went on the stage at age sixteen, acting the part of a nun. I can only imagine how this upset my grandparents, who were observant Jews. I think about what Lois told me about my grandmother. Do I dare ask Aunt Mary about that horrible time? I doubt if I ever would, but certainly not here.

The cigarette case is a gift from Freddie, who can't marry Aunt Mary until his mother dies. I have overheard conversations in our kitchen about this. Freddie's family disapproves of Aunt Mary because she had been married three times and because she had been a chorus girl. She was in a musical spectacular, the *Ziegfeld Follies*. I've seen a picture of my aunt walking down a curved staircase wearing a strapless, white sequined dress and carrying a large plumed fan. The dress has a long slit up the side, exposing her lovely, long legs. There are other beautiful showgirls in the photo, dressed just like my aunt.

"Aunt Mary, what happened to that photo of you when you were a showgirl in the *Ziegfeld Follies*?" I ask, trying to make conversation. She answers me as she waves to a couple walking into the room. Now I know why she chose a table in the middle of the room. She wants to be seen.

"Oh, I tore it up. Freddie didn't like it," she replies, waving to someone else.

I've heard my aunts say in a hushed voice that Freddie's mother calls my aunt Mary a kept woman. I'm dying to ask my aunt where she is kept. Kept in her apartment at the Park Lane Hotel on Fifth Avenue? Where she spends her days making herself glamorous for evenings at nightclubs with Freddie. That is what she must do to stay kept—stay glamorous.

Aunt Mary fits in with these famous and successful people although she has had no more than a fourth-grade education. I wish I could ask about her unusual life, or about my concerns. I get tongue-tied when I'm with her. I know she cares about how people look and dress, about how she looks and dresses, but I also know she cares about her family and me as well. She's generous with all of us. But at thirteen I'm old enough to know that I don't want Aunt Mary's life.

The smoke and the Jasmine scent of her perfume, "Sortilege," created by Sherman Billingsley, overcomes me. I stifle a cough. "Your mother is doing so well. It's as if she was never in an accident."

"That was a frightening night, Aunt Mary, but she's perfect now." I look around the room. "Are there any celebrities here this afternoon, like Lucille Ball? It would be great if I could tell my friends I saw a famous person." This is the kind of conversation I can have with my aunt. Maybe because of the way she dresses, or maybe because of how she makes me feel, she's a stranger to me even though she's my aunt. I can't be myself when I'm with Aunt Mary. I just can't!

"You mostly see the celebrities at night in the Cub Room," pointing to a separate room. She scans the club for people I might know. "There's Bert Lahr sitting at the bar."

"Wow! The cowardly lion in *The Wizard of Oz*," I shout out. "Sitting at the bar!"

"Don't shout, dear," she cautions me, putting her fingers to her lips.

The waiter brings our food. Covered in a tub of gravy, the hamburger looks juicy. I'm hungry, but I'm afraid to eat it because the gravy could drip on my clothes, and I would embarrass Aunt Mary. I take a small bite and try very hard not to drip the gravy, but a little bit splashes on the white tablecloth. I move my plate over to cover the stain.

"I guess I'm not that hungry," I say, hoping Aunt Mary doesn't hear the growls from my stomach. I reach for a forkful of creamed spinach.

She smiles, and hands me a large box dressed in a pink satin ribbon. "Here's your birthday present." Inside the box, swaddled in pink tissue paper, lies a hand-embroidered ice-skating costume. The short black velvet skirt is lined with red satin.

"Thank you so much, Aunt Mary. This is beautiful," I say, forcing a smile and hoping I don't have spinach caught in my metal cap. Last birthday, Aunt Mary bought me a white ermine cape and muff. No one in my neighborhood wears stuff like that, not even on Halloween.

A photographer stops by our table. Aunt Mary asks me to scoot closer to her so the photographer can take our picture. We will be frozen in time in this photo taken at the Stork Club—I on my thirteenth birthday, Aunt Mary, the hamburger in its tub of gravy, and the stork with a red rose in a beaker. The camera will capture us for *posterity*. My aunt instructs me, "Don't forget to smile for the camera." Trying to hide my metal tooth, I half-smile.

After lunch, I ask, "Do you think I can take the stork and the matches home?"

"Of course you can, dear," my aunt says. "With the photo it will be a nice memory of our lunch together." I spill the water from the beaker into my water glass, wrap the rose in my hanky, and tuck the stork and the matches in the box with the ice-skating outfit and the pink satin ribbon.

I'm relieved when I see Charlie waiting to drive us home. He drops my aunt at the hotel and then drives me uptown to my apartment. I can't be alone with Aunt Mary any longer. I don't fit into *her* Stork Club, and I don't want to.

Back in our apartment, I tear off my uncomfortable clothes and slip into a T-shirt and dungarees. Dragging the stepladder to my parents' bedroom, I plant the box with the ice-skating outfit next to the box holding the ermine muff and cape. Then I change my mind, leave only the pink ribbon in the box, and hang the outfit in my closet. Aunt Mary knows another thing about me—I like to ice-skate. I wouldn't wear this outfit when I skate with my friends at the Wollman rink in Central Park because we wear dungarees and our wool sweaters with reindeers on them. But I could wear Aunt Mary's present when I go ice-skating with my parents at Rockefeller Center, where lots of figure skaters wear fancy costumes.

I display the stork on the kitchen table and vow to buy a rose every now and then to put in its beaker. I rewrap the rose in tissue paper and stick it in my Webster's dictionary on the page with the word *posterity.*

Looking back on the afternoon, I decide it wasn't all that bad. None of my friends lunch at a famous nightclub on their birthday, and none of my friends have such a glamorous aunt. Out of the hand-me-down itchy suit, away from Aunt Mary and the well-dressed people and stuffy waiters at the Stork Club,

I feel giddy. I jump up and down, shouting to my image in the mirror in our dining alcove, "You drove home in a limousine, you ate lunch at the Stork Club, and you sat at a table with a beautiful former *Zeigfeld Follies* dancer who just happens to be *your* aunt."

The phone rings. It's Karen. "Well, did you see anyone famous?"

"I sure did," I brag. "I saw the Cowardly Lion sitting at the bar."

May 13, 1950—the Park Lane Hotel
Dear RR:

How come some people make me feel picayune and unlovely? I should have more confidence in myself. I should be like Jo in *Little Women*. We have much in common—our names are almost the same, we're tomboys, we like to write, and we have an aunt who is judgmental. I know Aunt Mary loves me and doesn't want to hurt me, but she does.

Chapter 16

Dress-Up in Aunt Mary's Clothes

Aunt Mary lives in a sumptuous hotel apartment, for which Freddie pays. Is my aunt a *kept* woman, as Freddie's mother describes her? I wonder if she enjoys being kept, and if she would like me to be *kept* when I grow up?

We lunch today in her apartment. From room service my aunt orders creamed spinach and a grilled cheese sandwich for me and a salad for her, which arrive on a cart the waiter brings up from the kitchen. I watch him remove metal covers from the dishes. A room-service lunch is so sophisticated!

Aunt Mary asks if I told my friends about lunch at the Stork Club, and did I show them my skating costume? I tell her they know all about our lunch and thank her again for taking me there. But I lie about the outfit. After we finish, I wheel the cart into the hall for the busboy to pick up. No dirty dishes for my aunt to clean!

"I'm going to take a bath," she tells me. She's going out with Freddie tonight. As she luxuriates in the marble bathtub, I explore her closet, which is almost as big as my parents' bedroom.

Her closet smells like the perfume worn by women shoppers in the boutique stores on Madison Avenue to which my aunt has taken me while she scouts for clothes. Fur coats in different styles and colors hang on one side. The creepiest fur is what my aunt calls a stone marten. It's made of small animal skins (I think they're mink), sewn together, nails still intact. Its jaw is wired to keep the mouth open in a frozen scream. The stone marten's eyes are made of glass and remind me of my doll Tousel's eyes, except Tousel's eyes don't scare me anymore. Also, the stone marten's eyes can not close. My aunt likes to drape the fur piece over her suits. I will never wear anything like that!

Hatboxes roost like birds above the cubbies. I remember a box containing a hat that looks like a bird's nest. I can't understand why a woman would wear a bird's nest on her head. Is that being feminine? I hope my aunt never gives that hat to Mother. Aunt Mary parcels out to her sisters clothes she no longer wears, usually last year's fashions, although how can fashion change that much from 1949 to 1950? I wonder when she'll start handing over her clothes to me. I hope she never gives me the stone marten. I would not keep that on top of my closet. I'd bury it in the woods.

Evening gowns and daytime dresses drape over cloth-covered hangers waiting their turn to go out on the town. I stroke two of the evening gowns—one is sparkly; the other is satin. I pretend I'm glamorous like my aunt, and these are the clothes I'll wear when I step out at night. But I'm finding it harder to pretend. When I was little I used to play dress-up. Aunt Mary would sit on the couch and laugh as I paraded in her clothes. I don't want to *play* dress-up anymore. I want to be dressed up. I want to *look* grown-up, not play grown-up.

Shoes fill cubbies on the entire back wall, yet I don't see one pair my mother could wear to work or to grocery shop. My aunt doesn't work anymore now that she's being *kept.* Also, I can't imagine Aunt Mary in a grocery store.

The rest of the shelves are filled with jewelry in velvet boxes, as well as silk underwear, scarves, gloves, and bags. I'm attracted to the glittery, beaded dress purses that sparkle and catch the light from the closet's overhead fixture. The bags sparkle like the jewels on Grandma Rachael's brooch. Movie actresses carry purses like these when they dine at supper clubs. I clasp one and picture sitting at a table in the Stork Club, my beaded bag next to the red rose in the beaker of the stork. Of course, my fingernails are lacquered red. I feel elegant and beautiful like Aunt Mary.

I inspect myself in the full-length mirror in the corner of the closet, and a gangling, ordinary-looking girl stares back at me. Even Aunt Mary wouldn't look good in the clothes I'm wearing: a plaid skirt, white cotton blouse, anklets, and penny loafers. My hair flops around my face. An idea pops into my head. I picture my aunt and me dressed in elegant look-alike outfits, strutting around the living room.

I strip down to my underpants and my Bobbie training bra. (I wonder why the smallest bra size in the world is called a training bra—training for what?) I stuff tissues in my bra.

Only a few months ago, I wanted to transform into a tomboy. Now I want to transform into glamorous. One minute I want to be a tomboy; the next I want to be pretty and feminine. My feelings bounce back and forth like the Spalding ball I throw against the wall in the schoolyard.

I discover a black, soft-wool dirndl skirt ending at my calves. I toss off my shoes and try on a pair of Aunt Mary's gold sandals, but my ankles fold over when I try to walk. Instead I choose a pair of black suede pumps and jam my socks into the backs to keep them on my feet.

I like the luxurious feel of satin, so I choose a white satin blouse. I slip on the blouse and tuck it in the skirt. It feels sumptuous against my body. The skirt slips off my waist, so I tighten the waistband with a safety pin. I shuffle over to my aunt's dressing table, notice "Fire and Ice" lipstick on the dresser tray, and apply some.

I dab "Sortilege" perfume behind my earlobes just like my aunt. I looked up *sortilege* in *Webster's Unabridged Dictionary* the other day, and it means sorcery or magic. I feel "*sortiluscious.*" I feel magical!

I admire myself in the closet mirror in my slinky blouse, soft skirt, and high-heeled shoes. I arrange my hair to one side and pin it back with a red silk flower hairpin. I feel glamorous. My aunt will notice I'm not a little girl anymore! She'll love me more when she sees how pretty I look. I run my tongue over my new porcelain cap and practice a full smile. Then I strike a pose—how I will stand when Aunt Mary comes out of the bathroom.

I hear the water drain from the tub, so I know I must move quickly. I search the closet for clothes similar to mine and discover another black skirt and pair of black suede pumps. I place the matching clothes on the bed and add a beaded bag for fun. Then I arrange myself. I plant my right foot in front of the left and lean back a little, place my right hand on my right hip, and glance downward with a knowing smile on my face. I'm not sure what I know, but I'm trying to look like the actress Lana Turner, or "Lah-nah," as Mother calls her. I can't hold this pose for too long without falling over. My aunt better come out of the bathroom soon!

The door opens. Aunt Mary floats into the bedroom, wearing a pink satin robe and pink high-heeled mules adorned with pom-poms. Her hair is wrapped in a terrycloth turban. She smells like lavender soap. Eyeing me up and down, she says, "Ruthie, those clothes are way too big on you. Aren't you too old for dress-up, dear?"

She scans the bed. "Why are these clothes laid out?" she questions me.

I want to tell her I thought it would be fun for us to dress alike; the busboy could take our picture posing together. We could show off our outfits to my father when he comes to pick me up, and maybe, just maybe, she'd tell me I look pretty. But instead I turn away from her. I feel unlovely and embarrassed. That feeling of confidence I had when I left Poppy's party on New Year's Eve flew away with the Stork.

"Oh, how sweet of you! Now I understand. You've laid out an outfit for me to wear tonight. But these clothes won't be dressy enough," she explains. "The beaded bag is a lovely choice, though, and you can help me pick out my jewelry," Aunt Mary continues, "but first you need to take off my clothes."

She takes a tissue and gently wipes the "Fire and Ice" lipstick from my mouth, not noticing the tears forming in my eyes. "I don't want you to get a lipstick stain on my blouse when you take it off."

I shuffle over to the closet. As I look at my half-dressed self in the mirror, I see the mink's glass eyes reflected along with mine. His mouth is open as if he's about to speak. I imagine him saying, "I feel as small as you do. I feel as picayune."

June 11, 1950–Jones Beach
Dear RR:

My father is loud and has a bad temper, yet my friends think he's fun to be with. Was he crazy to go to the beach before the sun even rises? Yet, the sunrise was sumptuous, the warm bakery rolls were heavenly, and I remember my mother's terrible sun blisters when she didn't wear sunscreen. I guess I don't always hate my father. But it's easier when I do. My father is my hardship, and a writer must have a hardship to overcome.

Chapter 17

The Volcano Goes to the Beach to Avoid the Sun

My father drags our red metal Coca-Cola cooler off its shelf in the linen closet, slamming it down on the kitchen table. I jump up. It's 3:00 a. m. and pitch-black outside. My father sure is being *rambunctious.* Jones Beach Sunday morning has begun.

He slams the refrigerator door and deposits food for the beach into the cooler. As he lights the burner under the coffee pot, a burned plastic smell floats out from the kitchen. My mother has burned the plastic handle more than once. Bang! The metal thermos hits the kitchen table before my father pours strong coffee into it.

"Everyone up! It's time to get ready to go!" my father screams. Karen slept over so she could join us at Jones Beach and hasn't budged during this entire racket. I had bet her a hot dog and a pickle that we'd leave at this hour. She thought I was demented.

"Ruthie, I owe you a hot dog and a pickle," she says as we start getting dressed. The white sailor cap she wears all summer is pulled over her hair.

"Try to be quiet, girls," my father instructs as he bangs his tackle box rambunctiously against the side of the elevator.

"The neighbors are asleep," my father loud-whispers to us as we drag our beach stuff down the hallway to the elevator.

We leave for the beach about 4:00 a.m. and leave for home around ten thirty in the morning. My father must beat the traffic. Of course we miss the sun, another of my father's goals. Sometimes we drive to the beach when it's pouring out! He likes to cast for fish in the ocean and meet my parents' friend Rita and her family, who arrive at the beach almost as early.

As we walk through the lobby, Karen whispers to me, "Your father's a riot. He looks so cute with his fishing rods, tackle box, and those waders in his hands." She grins at me, "Do you notice how his mustache moves when he speaks, but sometimes I don't understand anything he says because he has sort of an accent." Few people understand him, I think to myself. Thank goodness for that, or he'd probably offend all of them.

The lobby is empty; no light seeps from under the door sills of the apartments. Outside, the glow from the street lamps and the full moon blanket the streets and our car as we stuff it with beach gear.

"This is so great, being out in the dark at this hour. My mother would never do this," Karen says, jumping up and down.

"That's because your mother is not insane," I whisper as I hop in the car. Karen slides into the back seat beside me.

"Boy, am I hungry. Are we stopping at Gideon's to get poppy seed rolls and danishes, the way you said you do?"

I nod. My stomach is growling too, although it's only 4:00 a.m.

We park outside Gideon's Bakery, which isn't open yet for customers, but the bakers let my father buy what he wants. He carries several white bags filled with hot baked goods. Mother hands Karen and me a napkin and a poppy seed roll to eat on the way to the beach. The rolls, just out of the oven, are moist and warm.

"Do you have another pair of waders, Mr. Treglia?" Karen asks. "I know how to fish. I can get the hook out of the fish's mouth, too! I learned in camp."

"No, but you can use mine."

"Thanks," Karen shouts back. She grins at me.

At this moment I hate Karen. I don't want her to like my father, and I don't want her to like fishing. I hate to fish. I hate bait. I can't imagine anything more disgusting than taking a hook out of a bleeding, dying fish's mouth, except for the fish that will bunk in our sink until my father guts and cleans them. Dead fish are even more disgusting than Aunt Mary's stone marten. At least the fur piece doesn't smell.

"How great! There's hardly any traffic," Karen says. Now they're chums. "I went to Jones Beach with my uncle and my cousin last summer. There was so much traffic. It took us hours to get there."

"No chance of traffic at this hour," my father screams to the back.

"Not much chance of sun either," I remark.

My father tells Karen that everyone is a stupe who leaves for Jones Beach later than four on a summer Sunday morning. Then he starts to call the bad drivers stupes. Next thing I know, Karen falls into this stupe-calling thing. Sometimes Karen and my father call a tailgater stupe at the same time. I think *anyone* driving at this hour is a stupe. I ignore the two of them and stare out the window

It's about five thirty when we arrive at Jones Beach Parking Lot Six. This is the least crowded section of the beach, because it's the farthest from the bathrooms, the food stands and the amusements (not that they're open now anyway). My father parks in the first space on the left, his favorite spot, as the beach is directly in front of the car, making it easier to unload.

At this hour *his* spot is always free. He backs into the space. Karen and I drag two lounge chairs, which must weigh fifteen pounds apiece. Then we struggle to carry an equally heavy beach umbrella. My father believes the heavier the better. He sets up the umbrella to keep us from getting a moonburn. Karen and I spread an old quilt on the sand.

After pulling on his waders, Dad totes his fishing rod and tackle box to the edge of the water. The tide is low, so he wades out a bit before casting. Karen and I are still wearing sweatshirts and pedal pushers over our swimsuits. The sand feels cold under my bare feet. I see headlights from another car pulling into the space next to ours. It's Rita and her family. They stay at the beach all day like normal people.

"Hungry, girls?" Rita asks us as she and Mother prepare an early beach breakfast. I think how scrumptious food tastes on the beach. Maybe it's the salt air and seashell smell of the ocean.

Karen and I bring Rita's two young children down to the shore to search for shells. My father joins us and swings the children around and around. I remember what it felt like when my father swung me. I remember diving off his shoulders into the waves. I wasn't scared because I knew he would be there to gather me up when I sputtered out of the foam.

When did I start feeling embarrassed by my father? When did I start not wanting to be with him? Was it when I stopped being a kid?

The sky is beginning to color up. The sun hugs the horizon. "Look at that sun, Ruthie. It's glorious," Karen says, pointing and beaming. I rarely see the sun rise. I usually sleep in the car until it gets light. I have to admit the sun is sumptuous as it wakes up out of the ocean. Everyone is quiet just watching, even my father!

Dad hands out thick white zinc oxide ointment. He reminds Mother that she always gets sun blisters. She puts some on her nose. Sun blisters? At six in the morning?

While Karen trots off to fish with my father (he's letting her wear his waders), I watch them stroll off together. I kick the sand as hard as I can, then turn around to join my mother and Rita. "You don't even like to fish," Mother says as she leads me to a chair. I listen to them gossip. She talks about her sisters. I can't imagine Aunt Mary on Jones Beach! Aunt Mary and sand just don't go together. Mother hands me a cup of milky coffee. I think about the taxi ride home from the movie and Mother's head bleeding, and I'm grateful she's here. I kiss her on the cheek.

Rita reels off a story about my father. "As I drove up my driveway I saw 'the thing.' A foul-smelling fishnet spread over my *entire* back yard, dead crabs and seaweed clinging to it. Our block smelled of dead fish for days."

Mother is laughing so hard she spills her cup of coffee.

"Your father had hooked a commercial fishing net!" Rita says to me. "He thought I could use it for one of my craft projects. I like to collect pine cones, sea shells, ..."

"And smelly fishnets covered with crabs?" I add.

"I didn't speak to your father again for weeks," Rita says.

Karen runs over to me and shrieks, "The tide's come in. Let's jump into the waves." I can't stay annoyed with Karen. After all, I could have joined them. So I gallop down the beach with her, and we dive into the waves.

As we dry ourselves off, the parking lot fills up. It's ten thirty, and my father barks it's time pack up our gear. It seems we've just parked. Karen and I lug the chaise lounges off the beach in time to see Dad work himself into an argument with a red-faced young man in a convertible who's waiting for our spot. "You're taking too long to pack up, Pop." the man shouts.

My father yells back, "I'll take my sweet time. I pack in a certain way." Dad is getting that tightness around his mouth. His lips are pasted together. I know that look. It's the just-before-the-volcano-explodes look. I brace myself for a shouting match, but Mother touches his arm, "Enough, Joe; not in front of the girls."

Still, he doesn't rush. The two men glare at each other. My father picks up the quilt and shakes it out away from the convertible. "If we weren't here I bet he'd shake the sand from the quilt in that man's face," I whisper to Karen.

"Can't we stay longer, Dad?" I plead, as I do every Sunday when we leave the beach. "Our suits are still damp, and Rita's staying." My father gives me "the look." Karen and I wrap up in dry beach towels and pile into the backseat.

We're sandy and sleepy. Dad positions the bucket with the fish he and Karen caught on the floor between us, lifts the cooler into the trunk, and slams it and the car doors. The red-faced man looks like a teakettle about to steam off its top. Dad ignores him. His face is red too, and not from the sun. As soon as we pull out, the convertible screeches into our spot.

"Mr. Treglia," Karen says, "I didn't believe Ruthie when she said you always start heading for home around ten thirty."

"Five hours at the beach is enough," my father shouts. "Always leave early to the beach to avoid the traffic. Always leave early to avoid the hot sun."

I shoot Karen a look of disgust.

"Your father is fun," Karen whispers to me. "My Dad's never any fun!"

"You only see your dad once a week, Karen. I have to live with the *Volcano* every day of the week."

Karen practically puts her face into the bucket of fish. "I caught that bluefish," she says, pointing to it. I try to avoid looking at her fish, which is staring at us with dull eyes. "Your father said he'll clean and bone it for my mother." I picture my father cleaning the fish in the deep part of our kitchen sink, where my friends and I used to bob for apples at Halloween with my father looking out for us. Some of the fish my father will freeze, and some he'll give to Mrs. O'Brien, still trying to make up for the spaghetti that landed on her. She sure gets a lot of food from apartment 4J.

We sleep until a few blocks from our apartment buildings. "Hey, come with me to *tar beach* on our roof," Karen suggests as my father backs into a space. "My sister and I made sun reflectors out of cardboard and tinfoil and rub iodine mixed with mineral oil on our faces and bodies. You can use one of our reflectors," she offers.

"Dad, may I go over to Karen's for a while?"

"Sure."

As we start to walk toward Karen's building, I think about the time we went to the beach with my cousin Lois and her friends on a summer Sunday morning. My father was angry because we didn't leave for Jones Beach until 10:00 a.m. It took us three hours to crawl there because of the traffic. We parked in the main parking lot in a sea of cars and had to lug all our beach stuff across the steamy parking lot.

The beach was crowded with people. The air reeked of fried food from the concession stands, and coconut sun cream lotion was sliding off the bodies of the sun worshippers. And all of us sunburned badly because we'd slathered on iodine and mineral oil to tan, instead of my father's zinc oxide.

I think twice about the tinfoil sun reflectors and the iodine and mineral oil. I double back to where my parents are unpacking the beach gear. "Mother, would you hand me Dad's zinc to take with me, just in case the sun's too strong?" Mother smiles as she hands me the tube.

June 20, 1950–the hideout
Dear RR:

Some of my happiest days have been when my Aunt Edith and Uncle Hy visit.

I especially enjoy spending time alone with Uncle Hy, even though he thinks I'm a pest. There are some adults in my life with whom I'm comfortable–Mother, Uncle Hy, Aunt Edith, and Miss Devaney, but some adults I'm not–Aunt Mary, Mrs. Stepp, and often my father. I feel especially bad feeling that way about my own father.

Chapter 18

Unc and Cromo

I scurry home after school every day this week to hunt for a new black Pontiac with its hood ornament of an Indian chief, Pontiac.

"Where's the fire, Ruthie?" shrieks Mrs. Hamft as I run past her. She's leaning on her pillow in her neighborhood watchdog pose wiping the sweat off her face with a man's hanky.

"My aunt and uncle should be showing up any day now. They're driving up from Miami," I shout as I hightail it toward our building.

Aunt Edith and Uncle Hy visit us every summer for two weeks. Their car is here! I fly into our building, trip on the entry step, and struggle to get the key into the lobby door. Bounding up the stairs two at a time, I clatter down the hall and lean on the doorbell, too impatient to fumble with my key.

Mother answers the door. I rush into the kitchen, where I know everyone will be squeezed around the table, drinking coffee and eating dark pumpernickel bread with sour cream. I jump into my aunt's arms, and she holds me for a while. My uncle gives me a big hug. Then he and my father move into the living room, sit in chairs, and fall asleep.

I stay in the kitchen with the women and pick up whatever family stories they allow me to hear. Each time I bring up Grandma Rachael, they change the subject.

I tiptoe into the living room to ask Uncle Hy to walk in the neighborhood, something we do every time he comes up north. But his mouth is open, and he's making a putt-putt sound. I stare at his round balloon-like face. A fringe of hair curls around the base of his head. When I was younger he'd let me comb his hair and force whatever strands I could gather into a ribbon.

My uncle wears short-sleeved shirts. Havana cigars peek out of his top right pocket. Uncle Hy used to blow smoke rings for me. He stopped doing that about three years ago. I guess he thought I was too old. I suppose that's true, but I miss those circles of smoke. Uncle Hy gave me an empty cigar box, which I use to store my keepsakes. That's where I keep Grandmother Rachael's brooch watch, the matchbox from the Stork Club, and other private stuff of mine.

When Unc wakes up, I ask if he'd like to go for a walk. We both know I mean a walk to Stein's candy store where he buys me comic books. I have in mind the Archie Double Digest. I like the main characters. Archie, with his freckles and big grin, chases Veronica, the rich, sexy, heartbreaker. She reminds me of the popular girls in school. Sweet Betty, whose blonde hair is pulled back in a bouncing ponytail, tries to get Archie to notice her. I like Betty because I want boys to notice me too.

But this time, before our trip to Stein's, I decide to show him the hideout. I've never taken him there before because it's our private place. Of course, I don't ask him to slide down the hatch. He's not that *agile*. Instead, we enter the woods through a path next to Fort Tryon Park. The path is steep, though, and filled with rocks, fallen branches, and bramble.

"Cromo," he says, "what kind of walk are you taking me on?" Cromo is his nickname for me. I think it's a Yiddish word that means little pest. He only calls me that when my friends aren't around! They'd start calling me that. "Can't we just walk in the gardens in the park like everyone else?" he asks me, out of breath.

Uncle Hy scrapes the top of his head as he ducks under a branch. "Darn it!" he exclaims as cigars tumble out of his shirt pocket. I help him pick them up and brush off the leaves. He shakes his head, but I see a smile forming.

"I'm getting too old for this." Uncle Hy growing old? I don't want to think about that. "Where are we going?" he asks, pulling out his handkerchief to wipe the sweat off his brow.

"I'm taking you to our hideout, Unc. I want to show you something special I share only with my friend Karen."

We struggle a little farther and arrive there. Uncle Hy sits down heavily on the tree stump and wipes again his sweaty face with his hanky. It's quiet here in the woods, except for the cars humming along the West Side Highway. A few days ago I had stashed two Hershey bars in the hollow of a tree, double-wrapped in wax paper and tinfoil. I know how much Unc enjoys Hershey bars. I hand him one of the bars, which feels too soft in its wrapper, and sit down on the other log. We lick the melting chocolate bars off our fingers. "You're still my Cromo," he says, laughing.

My uncle lifts himself off the tree stump with some difficulty, stretches, and falls back on the log. He and Aunt Edith have no children. I think of them as my second parents. I know I'm more than a niece to them—more like the daughter they only get to see in the summer.

For a while my uncle and I listen to bird songs and squirrels playing in the tree branches. "Karen and I change into our tomboy clothes after school and race down here so we can be alone. Only we know about this hideout."

"I'll keep it a secret," Uncle Hy says with a wink.

Suddenly I feel sad, the way I did with Karen when I realized that we'd be going to different schools this fall. "I'm scared about going to high school in September. I've been in PS 187 for nine years, starting in kindergarten. Maybe I won't fit in."

"I'm not sure I like the idea of you growing up either. I wish you could stay a little girl, stay my Cromo." We don't speak for some time, and then he says, "Change is scary, Ruthie, but after awhile you'll get used to a new school, and it won't be so frightening."

Uncle Hy takes a cigar out of his pocket, bites off one end, and lights it. I give him a look; his eyes twinkle, and he slowly blows a whole bunch of smoke rings for me. I watch them change shape as they float away. Unc stomps out his cigar in the dirt. We begin to walk back the way we came. This time he ducks when he sees low branches. I pick up a few of his cigars along the path.

"Just like Hansel and Gretel leaving bread crumbs along the way to help them find their way home," I remark, giggling.

That evening, I tuck the Archie Double Digest comic book, which we bought after our visit to the hideout, under my pillow. When my aunt and uncle visit, they sleep on the sofa bed in the living room, and I sleep on the two club chairs pushed together, which keep slipping apart. I can't sleep because I'm too excited. Aunt Edith and Uncle Hy are here; I graduate from the eighth grade in four days, and we'll all drive down to Miami shortly after graduation.

I wonder why I never bring my father to the hideout. He's much more agile than my uncle. Maybe it's because my father would slide down the hatch, and someone I know might see him. Maybe it's because he would rearrange things. He'd take away my knife, saying it's too dangerous. He'd be figuring out how to make the logs into real benches. And he wouldn't let me help him do that. He'd have to make the benches himself. He tells me what to do or what I shouldn't do all the time—the way he did when I threw spaghetti out the window. He could never sit still on a log, quietly, without talking, as Unc and I did. And most importantly, he wouldn't understand why this hiding place is so important to Karen and me.

I wish my father was more like my uncle, and I wish I didn't feel that way.

June 24, 1950—driving to Miami

Dear RR:

I did not expect my first car ride to Miami to disturb me so much. Miami was summer with friends; Miami was palm trees, hot white sand, and pounding waves; Miami was Aunt Edith's breakfast popovers. Now the city is part of the South we drove through, the South where not all Americans are welcome. I'm still going to write the essay on "What It Means to Be an American." But the drive changed my mind about what I'm going to write.

Chapter 19

Negroes, Jews, and Dogs

My parents and aunt and uncle attended my graduation and didn't laugh at my graduation dress with the uneven hemline the way my friends did. They claimed they enjoyed hearing us sing the school song:

> *We suggest*
> *It's the best.*
> *You'll agree*
> *When you see*
> *PS 187*

It sounded out of tune even to me.

After graduation we went for an early dinner to celebrate. I wore my dress and corsage. At home, I pressed the white tea roses between the "gradus" page of my Webster's dictionary. Then I tossed the graduation dress on the top of the closet next to the ermine stole. It's getting crowded up there with clothes I'll never wear.

This is what my aunt and uncle wrote in my graduation autograph book.

"I'd like to say something clever, something entirely new—but all I can think of, darling, is, sweetheart, I love you. May life be good to you! Aunt Edith."

"You're the world to your mother and dad; to your uncles and aunts you're the tops, but to me you're the best, even though you're a pest, I wouldn't have anything better. Unc."

They'll be staying with us a few more days until we drive to Miami, then we spend the rest of the summer in their duplex. After two weeks, my father will fly home—Mother two weeks later. I leave in August, before the hurricane season. This time we'll drive down in the new Pontiac instead of taking the train.

My father packs my clothes so they don't get crushed. I'd dump everything in my case, sit on it to close, and iron whatever is wrinkled. But I've learned not to argue with my father about everything.

My suitcase has red-and-black stripes on its hard top, dividing the middle like a road. I'd like to own a makeup case, like Mother and Aunt Edith, but I don't need one just for the light pink lipstick I wear now.

After the suitcases and the Coca-Cola cooler are in the trunk, we're on our way. I dump a bunch of Archie comic books and some Nancy Drews on the floor in the backseat. Grandma Rachael's brooch is tucked safely away in my Bakelite handbag, a graduation gift from Aunt Edith. Mother, my aunt, and I sit in the backseat. I'm stuck in the middle, wedged between two sweaty arms. Mother and Aunt Edith are wearing halter tops, and I'm wearing a cotton drawstring peasant blouse like the teen models wear in *Seventeen* magazine.

My father is in a bad mood because it's 6:00 a.m., and he wanted to leave at four to avoid rush-hour traffic. He screams out the window, calling any driver who cuts him off a stupe.

"Dad," I say, "call the stupes *addlebrains* instead. Addlebrain means stupid."

"I don't like that word. I like stupe." We take a lunch break at a roadside rest area. By nightfall, we're hungry, hot, and tired. At a hotel in Rocky Mount, North Carolina, Dad marches to the front desk to register, and I tag along to see what it looks like. I've never slept in a hotel before, and I'm in awe of the sumptuous lobby. As I glance around, I see a large sign posted on a bulletin board:

"WE DO NOT PROVIDE ROOMS FOR JEWS OR COLOREDS"

Before I can point out the sign to my father, the desk clerk asks, "Sir, what is your religion?" I look back at the sign. Is that dumb clerk going to say that my family can't stay at this hotel because we're Jewish? Do we look Jewish? I stare at myself in a mirror in the lobby. I look like me. What *does* Jewish look like?

I don't know much about my father's background, but I do know he's *not* Jewish. He doesn't say that. Instead he glares at the clerk, who looks down at his guest register. "None of your business," Dad snaps. "We would like two rooms—one with a cot." I see a vein bulging on his forehead.

The clerk leafs through his register. "Sir, there are no vacancies," not looking up. "Try the Howard Johnson motel down the road."

My father continues to glare at the clerk, who has now turned away. Dad trudges back to the car. "*There are no vacancies!*" he shouts. He slams the car door so hard the windows rattle.

"There are so vacancies," I shout out. "Look!" A flickering red neon sign at the beginning of the driveway announces, "VACANCIES."

How come there are no vacancies for us?" I know the answer. It's because we're Jewish. But I don't understand the reason. No one answers me. I continue asking anyhow. "Why ..." but my mother puts her hand on my knee, and I stop. So Jews and Negroes aren't wanted everywhere! Could what happened to my friends in Europe happen to us here? I am both angry and afraid but disappointed too. That hotel was beautiful! I was so excited that we were going to spend the night there. Even Aunt Mary would stay in that hotel. But she couldn't either.

We head to the Howard Johnson motel and check in without any questions from the clerk. Then we drive to a nearby diner. A large platter of greasy southern fried chicken is placed on our table. Dad doesn't complain about the chicken or hand it back to the waiter, which is what he would usually do. If he didn't look like my father, I would think someone else is sitting in the booth. No one talks about the sign in the hotel and being turned away by the desk clerk. Do they think that not talking about it will make me forget what happened? If they do, they're wrong.

We return to the motel in silence. My aunt and uncle walk to their room, my parents and I to ours. In my cot, lying on my stomach with my flashlight, I don't feel like reading the Archie comics or the Nancy Drews.

In South Carolina, we stop at a general store for lunch food and Cokes. Next to the store slumps a rundown roadhouse with some old trucks parked in front. The *N* in 'VACANCIES' is not lit up in the neon sign for Clark's Motor Court. Several rusty cars are parked outside the sad-looking cabins, which look as if they'd fall down if you lean too hard on them. Nearby another sign in larger letters declares:

"For Colored Only."

The motor court gives me the creeps. The wood cabins are covered in moss. A damp smell from the shanties float over the dirt ground surrounding them and reaches us on the tarred driveway of the general store. I was glad when we went inside our car.

As we drive away, I say, "That sign means we can't stay there because we're not colored." Mother puts a damp arm around me and pulls me toward her. "That's the way it is here."

She's quiet for a minute, and then says, "When I was growing up in Ottawa, we were scared to go to school alone. Some of the Canadian boys used to call us names like 'kike,' a bad word for Jew, and throw things at us."

"But isn't that why Grandma Rachael left Romania—to get away from prejudice and violence against Jews?" Mother sighs and nods. "There's always going to be prejudice."

My aunt adds, "Lots of things are different in the South." Then she tells me about a sign she saw on a motor court in Florida that said, "No Negroes, Jews, or Dogs."

"At least we come before dogs!" I mean it as a joke, but as soon as I say it I know it's not funny.

I ask to sit between my father and my uncle. I feel safer up front with them. We drive on Highway One, a two-lane, two-way road. I notice cabins along the road that look like they should have fallen down years ago, but I see that people still live in them.

The attendant at a gas station gives us a free frosted soda glass. Would the owner of that gas station give one to Negro customers? Would he even let them buy gas? And what about us? How would he treat us if he knew we are Jewish? I never felt *different* before, but now I do.

The next morning, wanting a hearty breakfast, we stopped at Mama's Pancake House. A smiling Negro woman, wearing a white apron over a gingham dress, advertises the restaurant's name. "I bet 'Mama' can't eat here," I say aloud. "And what about us, if they knew?"

"I don't want to talk about it anymore," my father says, chewing his pancake. He always has plenty to say about everything. This time, when I want to know what he thinks, he has nothing to say!

Later we stop at a grocery store in Georgia to pick up lunch food. Dad seems very uncomfortable. Scared, in fact. My dad, scared! He's ... wacky ... angry ... loud! But scared? The only other time I remember seeing him scared was the cab accident, but that was different. He drives very slowly, never passing a car until we're out of the state, even the old broken-down trucks that putter along at ten miles an hour. "Dad," why are you driving so slowly behind those stupes?"

"I don't want to get a speeding ticket or have anything to do with the Georgia police."

Then he does something he hardly ever does. He tells me a story about when he was a kid hitchhiking down South and made a friend, a Negro boy. To earn money, they scrounged up used golf balls and sold them to golfers at a discount. One day they were arrested in Georgia for being together on the golf course. They were thrown in jail because it was against the law for white and colored to be together on a golf course.

"Maybe you should have been arrested for stealing golf balls, not for being with a Negro boy."

"The Georgia police only cared that we were together."

I'm actually carrying on a conversation with my dad. I can't believe he's been in jail. "Why did you run away? Didn't your parents try to find you?" I know my father would speed down the highway to find me if I left home.

"Didn't your parents care ...?" I start to ask, but my father cuts me off.

"I ran away from home. I don't want to talk about it anymore."

We eat our lunch in the car. When my father says, "Let's drive straight on to Miami," no one argues with him.

As I look for the bathroom at a rest stop, four signs above the doors jump out at me:

"White Men"
"White Women"
"Colored Men"

"Colored Women"

The water fountains are marked "white" and "colored" as well.

Whenever we stopped at a gas station or a general store I bought a pennant from the state we're traveling through to put on the inside of my clothes closet. I fling the Carolinas, Georgia, and Florida pennants into a trash can. Last summer Lois and I traveled to Miami by train. It was different when I viewed the South through train windows. I'm sorry my aunt and uncle bought a new car. I'm sorry I'm seeing an America that scares me. I've got a lot to think about.

We stop at a nice-looking restaurant near where my aunt and uncle live. The dining room is divided by a partition. The side facing the parking lot is run-down. I notice a table with Negroes, in uniform, on that side. In fact, everyone on that side is colored. The hostess ushers us to the other side of the partition, a lovely part of the restaurant facing a small pond. "Uncle Hy, what's going on here?"

"Well, honey, we're in the white section of the dining room. Dividing the restaurant is one way the South enforces the Jim Crow laws."

"Who's Jim Crow?" I ask. This is a guy I certainly don't want to meet. Is he Hitler's American cousin? And why didn't we learn about him in school?

Unc explains that the name Jim Crow came from a popular song in the South called "Jump Jim Crow." "Jim Crow has become a symbol some people in the South use to say that Negroes are inferior to whites." He pauses and takes a sip of his coffee. "That's why there are laws to keep the races apart."

"Well, they're hateful laws!"

I can barely eat my hamburger. "Colored soldiers fought for all people. I don't understand why they're considered inferior here."

"Two years ago," Unc tells me, "President Truman signed a federal law against lynching and ended discrimination in the military service. He said not all groups enjoy the rights of citizens. He felt the same as you."

"I remember that speech," Aunt Edith says, "because he spoke on the steps of the Lincoln Memorial."

"I don't remember learning that. What's lynching?"

"Enough questions, Ruthie," my father says in a tired voice. "I want to enjoy lunch."

Back in the car, I'm about to ask again about lynching. "But ..." Aunt Edith places a finger on my lips. I sulk all the way to Southwest Ninth Street, where my aunt and uncle live.

My aunt has rearranged her part of the duplex to make room for us. My cot is in the dining alcove across from the kitchen. The dinette set crowds a corner of the living room. My parents sleep on the sleeper sofa in the living room. I can't wait to shower.

I take so long in the shower everyone begs for me to get out. I soap and soap and still don't feel clean. I wonder if Negroes scrub themselves to try to get white. But I know they can't, any more than I can wash away being Jewish. It takes me a while to fall asleep. My mind is spinning like Dorothy's house, and tumbling around it are shanties, hateful signs, and soldiers marching. I want to be a child again in Aunty Em's kitchen, but it's too late. I've lost my childhood innocence, and the wizard is a fake and can't get it back for me.

July 31, 1950—Miami
Dear RR:

So much has happened this vacation, starting with our drive down south. I learned there are many different worlds to live in: my little world, of course, but also a world where you're restricted because of the color of your skin or your religion. There are joyful, safe worlds, and tragic, dangerous worlds. So far I've lived in both. The joyful world I've lived in this summer started with the teen center and meeting a boy named Frank.

Chapter 20

Grandma Rachael's Candlesticks

This summer boys enter the picture. It's off-limits for me to date, but I can go to the teen center on South Beach where the kids hang out. My uncle drops me off around 7:00 p.m. and picks me up before 10:00 p.m.

A couple of weeks ago a boy walked over and introduced himself. "Hi, I'm Frank. I've noticed you before."

I almost blurted out, "You noticed *me!*" But I caught myself and said, "Hi! I'm Ruthie."

"Mona Lisa," a Nat King Cole recording, was playing, and Frank asked me to dance. I had to tilt my head back to speak to him, and stand on my toes to dance. I nearly lost my balance because Frank is so tall. He has dark hair, which falls onto his forehead, and a smile that lights up his face. He has just finished his freshman year at Miami Beach High.

Tonight, Frank and I walk and talk on the beach, holding hands. The moon skips ripples of light over the ocean. I race him down to the water's edge. The rough surf rolls over our feet, spraying our clothing.

We stop under a palm tree, and Frank bends over to kiss me. This is my second kiss, if I count one from Larry in the stairwell of our building. But with Larry, I didn't feel warm all over, and my knees didn't buckle under me the way they do now. Frank and I lose our balance and land in a heap on the damp sand, laughing. "Your hair is beautiful, so shiny," Frank says, stroking my hair as we lay on the sand. Frank kisses my neck. I touch his shoulders. How strong he feels! I can't stop myself from touching his cheek. I feel tingly all over and pull him closer, but he pulls away and helps me to my feet. I'm confused. He puts his arm around my shoulder and leads me back to where the kids are dancing. "I'm afraid we'll go too far. You're only a kid."

The next day at lunch, I wonder whether I should tell Aunt Edith about Frank. I take a bite of my sandwich.

"Aunt Edith, I've been meeting a cute, very tall boy named Frank at the teen center." She takes a napkin and wipes off a bead of sweat that always appears above her lip.

"Oh!"

"I danced with him, and we walked on the beach … and … and …" I feel a little funny about completing the sentence, but Aunt Edith says, "and he kissed you."

I wonder how she knows. I feel warm all over again just thinking about last night. I didn't want her to know how it made me feel because I wasn't sure myself.

She smiles at me, taking a sip of her soda. "Don't you dare tell your uncle," she says. "Herbie is always calling here. He has a real crush on you." Herbie's mother is a distant relation of my uncle.

"I know. Look at this!" I grab a photograph Herbie had mailed to me. A forest of black, curly hairs has sprouted on his chest even though he's just fourteen. He shaved the letter R onto his hairy chest, signing the photograph, "Love always, Herbie." My aunt and I can't stop laughing. I tell her how I cringed when I saw him in a bathing suit last week at the beach with the R on his chest. "I'm keeping this picture to show my friends back home."

As we eat lunch, we listen to the radio. Warnings are being broadcast to prepare for a possible early hurricane. There is a tropical storm brewing in the Caribbean that may move up the eastern coast toward Florida.

"Remember when I called hurricanes '*hurrycanes*'?" I ask my aunt. She nods, smiling.

"I know you think being in a hurricane would be exciting, but hurricanes are dangerous. Often people are killed or hurt, and there's terrible damage to property."

"What's the worst hurricane you remember?" I ask as we clear away the lunch dishes.

"The worst hurricane?" We go into the living room, and I curl up on the couch. Aunt Edith sits down in Uncle Hy's faded green chair. "Probably the one when we lost our power for over two weeks."

"That must have been scary," I say, picturing the house and street in total darkness.

"It was. We knew we'd lose our electricity, so we stocked up on candles, flashlight batteries, and Sterno stoves."

"You must have stocked up on food."

"We always keep a supply of canned goods and bottles of water on the highest shelf in the linen closet," my aunt says, opening the closet door as I follow her. I stand on my tiptoes for a closer look. I spot two candlesticks.

"Whose are those?"

"They were a wedding present to Grandma Rachael. That's why she brought them from Romania."

Using a small ladder to drag them off the shelf, she places the candlesticks on the table in the living room. Grandma Rachael's candlesticks—all the way from Europe! I find it hard to breathe. The candlesticks are about a foot tall, simple in design. They look like tapered table legs resting on pushed-in pie-plate bottoms. I picture the candlesticks, wrapped in a blanket, crossing an ocean. I picture the candlesticks on the dining room table in the boarding house in Canada. After slowly rubbing my hands over them, I lift them up. "They're heavy!"

"They're solid brass."

"Grandma carried them such a distance," I whisper. My aunt nods. Sunlight from the window spreads over the candlesticks. I start to cry.

"Ruthie, what's the matter?" my aunt exclaims. She folds me in her arms.

I can't help myself. Everything Lois told me about my grandmother pours out. I tell my aunt how I look at Grandma's photo every day and how I feel close to her and how much I feel the loss of never having had her for a grandmother. And, feeling a little embarrassed, how I talk to her photo, even asking her to watch over her daughter the night Mother had the cab accident.

I run to my purse and bring the brooch watch Lois gave me for my birthday.

My aunt fondles the watch the way I fondled the candlesticks. She whispers, "This was a gift from your grandfather. I believe it was for their silver anniversary." She places it carefully on the table and stares out the window. Does she see herself back in Canada? Maybe she's remembering an ordinary Sabbath evening, the family gathered around the table, white candles anchored in the candlesticks, and Grandma wearing her brooch watch, its jewels glowing in the light from the candles. Why do I want to be part of this? There's a longing for a past I've never known that is part of my present.

"She would have loved you," my aunt says. I beg her to tell me more about my grandmother.

"Grandma Rachael wanted to forget the old country. She wanted everything modern, how she spoke and dressed, and the furniture she bought for the boarding house. She was happy to be living in Canada, where she didn't have to be afraid of a knock on the door. Friday night meant a lot to her.

That was when the family gathered together, and sometimes some of the boarders and relatives new to Canada. We scoured the house every Friday to prepare. She was an excellent cook. I still remember wonderful smells from her kitchen." Just like Mother, I thought.

Taking a deep breath, I ask, "What was my mother like after ...?" My aunt finishes my sentence, "after she found our mother?" I nod. "So you know everything?"

"Lois told me."

"Your mother was in a bad way. She wouldn't leave her room."

Then I realized not only Mother lost Grandma Rachael, but my aunt did also. "Oh, Aunt Edith!" I cry out, putting my arms around her. "Grandma Rachael was your mother too. I never thought ..." We sob together in front of Grandma's candlesticks and watch.

We talk all afternoon. She tells me that Iasi was near the Russian border. The Russian soldiers, Cossacks, often raided the countryside. "We were forced to leave because of their pogroms," my aunt explains, rubbing her hand over Grandma's candlesticks.

"Thank goodness you weren't in Romania during the war," I say. My aunt tells me at the beginning of World War II about thirty-four thousand Jewish people were living in Iasi. Now there are less than six hundred. As far as she knows we have no relatives left in Romania.

Now I understand why no one wants to talk about the past. Maybe that past is why my family stopped following Jewish traditions.

It's getting toward dinnertime. A heavy rain sweeps over our side of the street, and we rush to close the window, locking out the breeze that cooled the room. "I'll save these candlesticks for you. You can use them when you have own home." My parents now celebrate Chanukah. When I have my own home, maybe I can bring back celebrating the Sabbath with Grandma's candlesticks.

Then my aunt and I prepare cheese blintzes for dinner using Grandma Rachael's recipe. After dinner, we listen to the weather report on the radio. The hurricane has swerved out to sea away from Florida.

Before bed, Unc eats the Hershey bar he keeps in the refrigerator, and drinks a glass of milk. "This chocolate bar didn't melt all over my hands," he says with a grin.

August 12, 1950—South Beach
Dear RR:

I can't wait to tell my girlfriends about this teen hangout. It's different from Karen's and my hideout. I know now we'll never go back there unless we return to show our kids the hatch we used to slide down when we were tomboys. I'm more interested in Frank than in sliding down hatches. I submitted the essay to the Daily Mirror. I want to read it to Frank. He's not childish like the boys, including Harold Meister, at Poppy's New Year's Eve party. Maybe they too have changed over the summer, but I don't care about them anymore. And I certainly don't care about Poppy. Her parents are sending her to a boarding school in England. They probably can't stand her either.

Chapter 21

Significant Conversations

Seeing Frank waiting for me at the teen center makes me feel tingly all over again. I'm going to miss him. But high school is beginning to close in on me. Whatever else I say or do this evening I have to ask him what the first year is like.

Frank sees me, takes my hand, and we walk away from the other kids down to the surf. "I want to ask you something." Frank nods. "My first year in high school is about to begin, and I don't feel ready. How was freshman year?"

"I mostly liked it."

"Mostly? That makes me even more nervous."

"I'm on the basketball team. It's a good team, nice guys. I think I can tell you this. You're different than the other girls around here. What I don't like is that we have no Negro kids in our school and, of course, none on the team. My parents would kill me if they knew."

"Knew what?"

"That my closest friend, Jack, is Negro. We sneak off and shoot baskets together. He's smart. He wants to be a doctor. His school is not as good as mine, but he can't go to Miami Beach High because he's Negro."

I remember at the start of my summer here, I boarded a bus to meet my friends. A sign on the bus startled me:

"COLORED PASSENGERS USE BACK OF BUS"

Surely this was on buses before, but why didn't I notice it other summers? Maybe I did this time because of all those addlebrained signs I saw on our drive down here. This was one too many, and I had to do something, so I sat in the back. The bus driver shouted at me to move, pointing to the sign. I didn't want to go to jail like my father, so I left my seat and moved to the front. Everyone was staring at me.

I didn't know how my friends felt about Jim Crow laws, but when they were shocked I tried to sit in the back, I knew. I also knew I could not feel the same way about them any longer. I tell Frank what I did on the bus. Frank is different. He cared.

"At least I did something, even if I couldn't change anything. You and Jack are changing things by being friends. But I worry that other kids who see you together might hurt you. Could you get arrested? My father did just for being with a Negro boy on a golf course."

"It is dangerous."

"Jack plans to be a doctor. What are you going to do when you finish school?"

"Our school motto is, *Let us be known for our deeds.* I want to go into politics to change things. How about you, Ruthie?"

I push the damp sand with my feet. "I've always liked to write. I'm going to join the *Cherry Tree*, the school newspaper, because I want to be a journalist. As a reporter maybe I can write about the things I saw that shocked me, things I wrote about in my essay."

"What essay?"

"An essay I submitted to a newspaper in New York for a citywide contest. The subject is '*What It Means to Be an American.*'" I reach into my beach bag and pull it out. "I brought it to read to you." We sit on a bench facing the surf. My hands are shaking as I read. Will he think I can't write? Will he think I was dumb to send it off?

What It Means to Be an American

I used to think that being an American citizen meant being free. Our Declaration of Independence in paragraph two states, "We hold these truths to be self-evident, that all men are created equal... that among these (rights) are Life, Liberty and the Pursuit of Happiness." I don't believe that was written only as a reason to free us from Great Britain. I believe it went further. These words were meant to establish how life should be in the new nation.

Driving from New York City to Miami, Florida, this summer, I learned some freedoms are denied to American citizens. I learned America is a country of yes and no. Yes to my father as an Italian American citizen—no to my father as a Jew. Yes to the Negroes when they serve in the armed forces so long as they were separate from the whites—no to the Negroes if they want to stay in a particular motel.

My family and I were turned away from a hotel only because we were Jewish. I saw signs trumpeting "No Jews or Colored" in bold black letters. Soldiers, still in uniform, sat in a separate part of the restaurant where we stopped for dinner. Negroes use separate bathrooms and water fountains, sit in the back of the bus, and attend separate schools. Are they not Americans? Are they so inferior to the white race that they cannot share the same space? Are Jews so different that they must live separately from everyone else, or be slaughtered as they were in Europe?

As I ask why there is so much cruelty and hatred in Europe, I also ask why the same is true in parts of America. This is the country that opens its arms to oppressed people from all over the world. Listen to the words of Emma Lazarus, a Jewish woman, carved into a tablet within the pedestal on which the Statue of Liberty stands, "Give me your tired, your poor, your huddled masses yearning to breathe free ..."

What can we do, what should we do, and what must I do? A start for me is to never judge people by the color of their skin, by their religious beliefs, or by their ethnic background. If we are really Americans we must speak out when we see injustice, through our words, our movies, our art, or the government we elect. Who knows? Maybe someday the president of the United States will be a Negro, or a Jewish man, or why not—a woman?

President Truman delivered a speech from the steps of the Lincoln Memorial on June 29, 1947, calling for state and federal action against lynching, prejudice, and intolerance. Full civil rights and freedom must be guaranteed for all Americans. "When I say Americans I mean all Americans."

It is the job of our president, our government, and "we the people" to be the keepers of the "blessings of liberty." That's what it means to be an American!

Frank frowns. "Jack and I went to see *Storm Warning* last night. Doris Day and Ginger Rogers are in it, but it's not a musical. It's a frightening movie about the Ku Klux Klan. We couldn't sit together. Jack sat in the balcony, and I sat in

120

the orchestra. It would make him feel good to know another white person is angry at the way he's treated."

"Do you think my essay could win? First prize is a week working at the paper. I want that so badly, but I had to write this even though I don't think it's what the paper is looking for. I love America, but I want to help make it better."

"The newspaper will probably find it too irreverent to print. But whether or not it wins, you can write. The best journalists write the truth."

"At least it was neat. No ink blots, cross outs, misspellings, or incorrect margins. My English teacher would be proud of me."

I've never spoken with anyone the way I've spoken with Frank. This may be the most important afternoon of my life. I want it to go on forever.

"The night is like a lovely tune ..." Billy Eckstine croons through a loudspeaker from the teen center.

"Beware my foolish heart..." The music floats over to the beach. Frank pulls me close. We slow dance to the music. I press my head against his chest, and he strokes my hair. He bends down to kiss me. I feel his tongue caressing my lips, and then slipping inside my mouth. What is this? I'm confused, but I don't want him to stop. What comes next?

"Take care, my foolish heart." But my heart is not taking care. It's pounding like the surf. Out of the corner of my eye, I see my uncle walking to meet us. I forgot he's coming early today. He bends down to pick up a cigar that has fallen out of his pocket. I jump apart from Frank. "There's my uncle!" Part of me wishes he hadn't come, but part of me is relieved. I wish I could have spoken to Lois about sex. I have a lot to learn and Virgie's cartoons certainly didn't help.

Frank squeezes my hand as he walks me part-way up the path.

"I'm going to try to visit you in New York. I have a cousin who lives in Brooklyn. Write me!" That's the last thing I hear him say.

I wave to him. "I will! I will!" I shout.

I'm quiet in the car. "Cromo," my uncle says, "I bet you're going to miss that boy. You're growing up, I see," and he squeezes my arm.

This summer I learned that America isn't always "the land of liberty and justice for all." We recite that in the pledge of allegiance every morning in school, but I never really heard the words until now. I'm proud to be an American, but there will always be a Jim Crow around the corner waiting for his chance to ruin something beautiful!

My aunt and uncle have been so understanding this summer, I feel guilty that I shared my essay with Frank but not with them. That's because they would be disappointed I didn't write the essay about my family and friends coming to America.

My grandmother, my father, and my friends have their stories. I have my own story to tell.

August 15, 1950—on the plane
Dear RR:

It's time to say good-bye. Good-bye to Aunt Edith and Uncle Hy. Good-bye to this summer in Miami, when I learned so much about the world and myself. Good-bye to Frank. Even if I never see him again, he will always be the first boy I really kissed.

Chapter 22

Good-Bye

Storm warnings blare over the radio, but this hurricane also has moved out to sea. I guess I'll never see one. But I remember my aunt's words that hurricanes are dangerous. Another childish dream I must let go. I have three days left before I fly home.

This afternoon, my aunt comes home with two large shopping bags from Mangles, the woman's dress shop where she works. "For you, to wear in high school. You're getting taller and filling out!"

I tear into one bag and pull out a teal-blue corduroy jumper with a matching belt, along with two mock turtleneck jerseys in different colors. A navy-blue wool skirt and a pink angora twin sweater set are in the second bag. My aunt has even included a small, pink paisley scarf. They're just like the back-to-school clothes in the teen magazines.

I kiss Aunt Edith and try on the new clothes. I stare at myself in the full-length mirror. They fit a lot better than clothes in Aunt Mary's closet, or that baggy suit I wore to the Stork Club. I've gained five pounds from the chocolate milkshakes I've been drinking. The "curse" hasn't blessed me yet, but I fill out a new AA Bobbie bra. I realize it's not important for Aunt Mary to like me in these clothes. I like me in these clothes!

The next day, I'm meeting my uncle for lunch. I take a bus downtown to Flagler Street and sit in the front, taking a quick glance at the Negro passengers jammed in the back of the bus. The bus stops near the men's shoe store where Uncle Hy works. He's helping a customer, who purchases wingtip shoes—a black and a brown pair, just like the ones he's wearing. "It's much easier to sell men shoes, Unc." My uncle nods as he rings up the sale.

Unc and I eat our lunch at a nearby deli. I peek at the sky through the deli's windows, and dark clouds whisk by. Across the street a man is boarding up his storefront.

"Why is he boarding up his windows? The hurricane is going out to sea."

"Sometimes hurricanes change direction," my uncle responds. "He's just being cautious."

I'd still like to experience a scary storm. "School doesn't start until after Labor Day. I could stay another week," I suggest, taking a bite of my hot dog.

"I'm afraid you'll miss school if it swerves and hits us." The overhead light in the deli highlights a lump on the side of his head. When we played miniature golf last week, I swung my golf club too wide and whacked him on the head. He sulked off.

"You know, Unc," I said, trying not to look at the swollen lump because I felt the giggles coming up, "when I was a little girl, I believed it when you told me you sold your hair to the air force to make parachutes." Uncle Hy looks at me and shakes his head. It's a look I know well.

"You're still my *Cromo*."

He walks me back to the bus stop. "I'm afraid you may not want to spend the summer in Miami next year."

"I'll always want to spend my summers here with you and Aunt Edith."

But I have a feeling he may be right. I used to count the days until I went to Miami. I still love the beach and the ocean, the palm trees, and the bright flowers. I love walking barefoot on the coarse grass. I love living in the duplex with my aunt and uncle. And now there's Frank. But the Wicked Witch lives in this city, too. I never saw her before, but now I know she's here. My summers in Miami will never be the same.

The day has arrived for me to leave Miami. We hardly speak on the drive to the airport. I think of Frank. I think of his kisses. Maybe he can visit over Christmas vacation. I'll teach him how to ice-skate at Rockefeller Center. I'll even wear my skating outfit from Aunt Mary. It does look professional, and now it should look good on me.

Aunt Edith and Uncle Hy walk with me to the beginning of the runway, just before the gate. We hug for a long time. My aunt says, "Write us. We want to hear about high school."

"Don't worry about high school. You'll find your place." Unc winks at me.

From my window seat, I see my aunt and uncle at the gate. I wave to them, and they wave back. The plane takes off. I look for them until they're too small to see. The sky is dark, and raindrops are running down the windowpane. It seems like the raindrops are also running down my eyes. My life is rushing ahead like Tousel caught in a strong wind. I couldn't wait to be thirteen, and now that I am, I think about being a little girl again when life was simple. But I know that part of my life is behind me.

I picture Grandma's candlesticks with the sun shining on them. Taking her watch out of my purse, I pin it to my blouse the way Grandma pinned it in her photo.

Soon I'll find out about the contest. But Frank's probably right. The *Daily Mirror* wouldn't publish an essay so critical of our country, even if they did think it is well written and neat.

This summer I had a boyfriend who liked my hair, kissed me, and thought I was different than other girls—a boyfriend who thought about important stuff. And then there's Herbie. Even though he's a jerk, he did shave an *R* on his chest. Wait until Karen sees that photo! I'm not Ruthie anymore. I want to be Ruth from now on, even though that's what my father calls me when he's angry.

Stroking Grandma's watch, I think of all she went through in her life. I don't believe in ghosts, but I do believe that the spirit of family lives on. I do believe I have inherited some of her courage. I'm not as afraid of attending George Washington High School now. I think I can find my place. I unpin her watch from my shirt, place it back in its velvet box, and carefully bundle it into my purse.

The pilot announces over the loudspeaker, "We're going to try to fly above the storm clouds," he says. "You may experience some turbulence." I'm not scared. I'm used to turbulence. I live with "the Volcano."

Final RR

Dear RR:

You have been my best friend for almost a year. Writing in this diary has helped me think about important stuff and record the last year before high school. I'm going to store you inside the ermine muff my aunt gave me for my twelfth birthday. Someday, when I'm older, I'll take you out and remember what it was like this year—the year I turned thirteen. Along with my grandmother's brooch watch, and someday her candlesticks, you are one of my prized possessions.

Thank you, RR.

Ruth

Discussion Guide

1. What concerns would a girl Ruthie's age have today?
2. How does today's social networking make your life different from Ruthie's?
3. Compare today's movies and movie stars with those of Ruthie's era.
4. Do movies influence you as much as they did Ruthie? If so, how?
5. Ruthie grew up in a time when television sets were just appearing in a few homes. What other electronic equipment was not yet invented or used in the early 1950s?
6. Choose a new word each month, and use it when you write, text, or speak to your friends.
7. Where and when were there pogroms in Europe?
8. When and how did Hitler come to power?
9. Were only Jewish people placed in concentration camps?
10. When and from what countries did immigrants go through Ellis Island?
11. How do immigrants arrive in America today?
12. What new immigration laws are being proposed now in Congress?
13. Where is "ethnic cleansing" happening today?
14. What else did President Truman say in his speech about discrimination in America? What were some of the Jim Crow laws?

15. Rent the movie *Storm Warning*. Use it as a basis for learning more about the KKK.
16. Which president passed the first civil rights laws? What were they? How were they enforced?
17. We still have discrimination in America today. What would Ruthie have done? What can you do?

Acknowledgments

I would like to acknowledge those who have helped me in the creation of this book: my first writing teacher, the esteemed author Patricia Reilly Giff, who first encouraged me to move forward; and my second writing teacher and later editor, Carol Dannhauser, who inspired me to turn a series of essays into a novel. Since the computer and I are not on friendly terms, I thank Mark Evens and Jeff Elster for their invaluable help, and, finally, my lifelong friend Carol Cohen for her memories and for the fun we had together as tomboys in Washington Heights in the late '40s.

I would especially like to thank my husband as my editor. He gave me hours of his time more than any professional agent. And he still takes out the garbage.

CPSIA information can be obtained at www.ICGtesting.com
Printed in the USA
BVOW07s0424141113

336219BV00002B/6/P